Diva

Also by Alex Flinn

BREATHING UNDERWATER

BREAKING POINT

NOTHING TO LOSE

FADE TO BLACK

ALEX FLINN

Diva

HARPERTEMPEST
An Imprint of HarperCollins*Publishers*

HarperTempest is an imprint of HarperCollins Publishers.

Diva
Copyright © 2006 by Alex Flinn
www.harperteen.com
Library of Congress Cataloging-in-Publication Data
Flinn, Alex.
Diva / Alex Flinn.—1st ed.
p. cm.
Summary: Despite her mother's objections, sixteen-year-old Caitlin
determines to pursue her dream of becoming an opera singer by
attending a performing arts school in Miami.
ISBN-10: 0-06-056843-7 (trade bdg.)—ISBN-13: 978-0-06-056843-6
(trade bdg.)
ISBN-10: 0-06-056845-3 (lib. bdg.)—ISBN-13: 978-0-06-056845-0
(lib. bdg.)
[1. Singers—Fiction. 2. Self-confidence—Fiction. 3. Interpersonal
relations—Fiction. 4. Mothers and daughters—Fiction. 5. High schools—
Fiction. 6. Schools—Fiction.] I. Title.
PZ7.F6395Div 2006   2005028765
[Fic]—dc22
CIP
AC
Typography by Sasha Illingworth
1 2 3 4 5 6 7 8 9 10
❖
First Edition

To Kevin and Laura

Thanks to Joyce Sweeney, Lara Zeises, Nancy Werlin, Marjetta Geerling, Toni Markiet, Catherine Onder, George Nicholson, and my family for their help and support. Special thanks to Marie Baker and the teachers and students at Marlboro High School in New York, for talking to me about Nick, Caitlin, boyfriends and girlfriends, why I needed to write another book about these characters, and for helping me put together what I wanted Caitlin's story to be about, and what I didn't want it to be about too.

*L*ots of girls I know call themselves divas. "I'm such a diva!" they say, as they're rubbing your nose in some five-hundred-dollar shoes their daddy bought them. But being a diva's a lot more than just being a rich grrrl. It's about singing, about getting flowers thrown onstage—about being brilliant. I plan to be a diva someday. But first, I have to get through this audition.

And—wouldn't you know it—there's a wad of phlegm stuck in my throat.

The scene: I'm in an auditorium with, maybe, fifty other wannabes, trying out for the musical theater program at Miami High School of the Arts. Goths sit with goths, punk rockers with punk rockers. The girl next to me has an eyebrow-ring and hair Jell-O–dyed acid red. Everyone here has something freaky about them . . . except me. I'm the one and only person here in a dress (which maybe *is* freaky).

And I bet I'm the only one here with gunk in my throat.

Don't think about it. But I can feel it lying behind my tongue like cafeteria spaghetti, at a life-changing audition. I clear my throat and Eyebrow-Ring Girl gives me a look and nods at the person onstage.

'Scuse me—I'll choke more quietly in the future.

I sneak another look at her. My cheerleader friends would say she probably isn't getting enough attention at home. But I think anyone who'd wear that outfit has to be cool, and I wonder what it would be like to *want* to be noticed.

Me, I'm all about not being noticed. I'm sixteen, and for the first fifteen, I was a fatgirl, invisible as they come. I was okay with that. Well, maybe not okay, but . . . used to it. But last summer, I went to fat camp and lost thirty-five pounds, and became (at least temporarily) a *thin* girl, a blond prettygirl. I actually made the homecoming court and dumped the hottest guy in school . . . and still became one with the walls most days.

If any of my friends knew I was here, auditioning for a performing arts school, *that* they'd notice. In a *bad* way. But I didn't tell them. I didn't even tell my mother. This is the first time in my life I've ever done anything all by myself.

There's a bunch of reasons for that.

First, my friends all want me to be like them—cheerleaders, homecoming queens. I thought by losing weight I *could* be like that. But now, even though I'm thin enough, I'm still not cheerleader material. Funny, changing how I looked didn't change who I *am*. I picture myself doing a pyramid or making up a cheer and . . . *oh, puke.*

"See anything interesting?"

Too late, I realize I'm still staring at the girl with the eyebrow ring. *I am a dorkus maximus.*

"Um . . . I love your hair."

"What are you doing?" she asks.

I stare at her. Is it *that* obvious I don't belong here? Is it the dress?

"For the audition? *Habla ingles?* What are you performing?"

"Oh . . . I sing . . . opera." I wait for her to laugh or make a snarky comment.

"Cool." She raises her pierced eyebrow. "You have one of those horn helmets?"

I make the face Mom calls my diva face—eyeballs up; trying not to snort. "Um, not yet."

"Sorry. It's just, you don't look like an opera singer. You're not . . ."

"Fat?" *No. Not anymore.*

The girl laughs. "That's not what I was going to say."

But I know it was. It always is.

The woman up front calls a name (not mine). Eyebrow-Ring Girl turns to look.

Opera is the second reason I'm here. I love it. Most people think opera is a weird thing. Probably so. But it's *my* weird thing—the one thing I'm really good at. Maybe good enough to get a dessert named after me someday (Peaches Melba was named after a diva) or maybe a town. Maybe even good enough to get into this school.

The biggest, hugest reason I'm here (*and* the reason I'd never tell anyone) is my ex-boyfriend. I need to go somewhere where everyone hasn't already heard the sad, sad saga of me and Nick. And also, where I don't have to see him every day.

I pop a cough drop into my mouth and make myself sit still for two whole minutes, until the girl who's auditioning finishes singing.

Omigod! What if I'm next?

"Sean Griffin," the woman up front calls.

I actually really, really wanted to be next.

I read a book about auditioning. It said the worst thing that could happen in an audition is that you don't get the part, so you have no money, so you can't buy food, so you die. Like . . . if you thought that the absolute worst thing that could happen at an audition was *death*, then you'd be less nervous about screwing up.

That so did *not* make me feel better.

"Here I am!" a voice sings.

The guy, Sean Griffin, is skinny and wears a purple unitard, which seriously clashes with his blond hair, and eyes so blue I can see them even from a distance. He looks older, and he's been standing with the teachers, so I thought he was an assistant or something. Guess he's just a suck-up. He walks onstage, plunks a Burger King crown on his head (Really!), and starts to sing.

Everything has its season. Everything has its time.
Show me the reason and I'll soon show you a rhyme!

As soon as he starts singing, I'm nervous. I mean, *more* nervous. Lots of people at the audition were good. But Sean Griffin is the first person who's like a professional, even in that geeky outfit. I now know why he was standing up there with the teachers, like he belonged there. He knows he's going to get in.

I wish I was confident like that. I know I'm good, but sometimes, when everyone's staring, I wonder if it's just some dumb idea, thinking I'm good *enough*.

He finishes singing, and the applause is wild. He smiles like he's used to it.

"Caitlin McCourt!"

Now, it's my turn. My throat feels worse. I wonder if it could be all in my head. Is there such a thing as psychosomatic mucus?

"Caitlin McCourt?"

"Here." I start toward the front of the auditorium.

Onstage, the accompanist says, "Hey, how about a bathroom break?"

"Oh." The teacher looks at her watch. "Okay. Caitlin, do you need an accompanist, or do you have a tape?"

I glance at the sheet music in my hands for *Phantom of the Opera*. But I've done the hardest part, I want to tell them, the standing up and walking down and having everyone stare at me in my too-cute dress part. I turn back around.

"I can play for her." The guy, Sean, is reaching for my sheet music.

"Oh, that's okay. I can wait. I wouldn't want . . ."

"No worries. I can play anything. I'm a great sight reader." He takes my book and flips it open to the page where I've had my thumb jammed for the past hour. "This?"

When I nod, he glances at the book. "Hard stuff."

"I can wait if you can't play it." Except if I sit now, I might never get back up.

"I meant hard for you. This goes up to a C above high C, doesn't it? That's way high. Are you that good?"

Wow, thanks. That really helps me feel less nervous.

Actually, I've had that C for over a year. I write down the dates when I add new notes to my range. High C was last March 13. Now I'm working on E-flat.

"Come on, Caitlin. It's Caitlin, right?" Sean puts his hand on my shoulder and guides me toward the stage. My legs are all shaking.

My legs always used to shake when I sang. It hasn't happened in a while . . .

Flashback: Me. Sixth grade. Looking like I might explode out of my jeans any second at middle-school orientation. I was with Mom (big mistake). I was signing up for chorus. The music teacher, Mrs. Hauser, said I could either go for Girls' Chorus—no audition required—or try for Concert Choir, which was mostly eighth-graders.

"Girls' chorus sounds fun. Right, Caitlin?" Mom stopped fiddling with the purple alligator clip in her hair and started toward the sign-up sheet on the piano. She was wearing hot pink size-one capris and a tube top. Doesn't everyone's mother?

"Wait. I don't want to be in Girls' Chorus. I mean, I do want to be, if that's all I can be in, but I want to be in Concert Choir. I mean, I want to try."

Mom had moved away from the sign-up sheet and was nudging me, all, "Caitlin, sweetie, there's an *audition*. That means you'd have to sing in front of everybody. By yourself."

"I know. I heard her. I get it."

"But honey pie, you can't sing by yourself in front of everyone. You're . . ."

Fat. I heard it even though she didn't say it. I heard her thinking it.

"You're shy . . . you've never sung in front of anyone in your life, dear."

"Can I try?" I asked Mrs. Hauser, not Mom.

"Of course you can."

"Are you sure, honey?" Mom said. "I have appointments. You heard what she said. It's all eighth-graders."

Mrs. Hauser stood there with an oh-god-don't-make-me-get-involved-in-this look. I faced Mom down for the first time ever.

"I'm staying." I took the pen from Mrs. Hauser and wrote my name on the audition sheet. I joined the kids in the corner, and Mom sat down.

When Mrs. H. called my name, I wanted to run. Mom was right. It was one thing to sing in my room. It was a completely 'nother thing to sing in front of fifty people—and not one of them looked like a sixth-grader. But I walked up, feeling like Snow White in the movie—pre-dwarves—when she's dumped in the forest and all those eyes are looking at her from the darkness. My legs were shaking so hard I thought I'd fall over.

I closed my eyes, opened my mouth, and started to sing.

The world didn't end. Halfway through, my legs stopped shaking.

I opened my eyes.

In *Snow White*, when the A.M. hours come, Snow realizes that the scary eyes in the night are really gentle woodland creatures. That's how I felt that day. The people in that room were looking at me, but not in a bad way. I'd never met them, but they were like friends. They wanted to know me because I was good. I was really good. At that moment, maybe I was even a little visible.

I made Concert Choir that day—the *only* sixth-grade girl who did, thank you very much—and since then I've made most things I've tried out for.

Here and now: My legs are shaking so hard I can barely stand, so I lean against the piano like those opera singers on PBS. I'm calm. Really. I breathe. You're good at breathing, Caitlin. Very good. You *practice* breathing for opera.

"Are you ready . . . Caitlin?" Sean says my name real soft.

I nod. If I could still close my eyes, I would. But of course, I'd look like a complete dork if I did that.

Right before the music starts is the quietest time in the world. I can hear other people breathing. Then my song. I can feel it in my body. It's too late to back out now. It's sing or be forever known as the girl who ran away in the middle of the audition.

Concentrate!

In the song, Christine's this opera singer who's possessed by the Phantom of the Opera. He sings through her, from inside her, making his voice come through hers. I try to feel the Phantom singing through me, locked inside me, making my voice climb higher, higher, until my muscles hurt from breathing. *Up!* I think, as I was taught, forcing the voice into my head, and through it all, I feel the Phantom inside me, hear his voice, screaming, "Sing, my Angel of Music! Sing to me!" like the voice on the CD. It seems so real, and my voice climbs higher, higher, and only when it gets to the highest note do I realize that the Phantom's voice *is* real; it's not just in my head. It's Sean Griffin's voice behind me at the piano.

I gasp out my last note, a high C, and it's over.

Then silence again.

Then applause. *Big* applause.

Sean grins at me from the piano bench. I grin back.

Okay. So I can, on occasion, rock.

Back in my seat, I listen to the fifth girl to sing "On My Own" from *Les Miz*. She's also the worst. I feel bad for her. Then the girl with the eyebrow ring, who does the witch's rap from *Into the Woods*, and who is so good I sort of hate her, and a six-foot-tall football player type who actually sings "I Whistle a Happy Tune" from *The King and I* badly while everyone tries not to lose it.

And then it's over. "You'll hear one way or the other next month," the director tells us. "Thanks for coming."

People start leaving. I want to say something to Eyebrow-Ring Girl, compliment her on how incredible she was, but she's already gone. I stoop to pick up my music.

"Hey," a voice says behind me.

I look up. It's Sean Griffin. People are walking out.

"Hi," I say. "Um, thanks for playing for me."

"No problem. You need a ride somewhere?"

I took the train here, and I have to take a bus home from the train station. But I can't get in a car with some guy I don't know, just because he's a good singer. With my luck with guys, he'll turn out to be a perv or a serial killer.

"Uh, no thanks," I say. "My mom's picking me up."

"Oh, okay." He grins. Up close, his eyes aren't really blue, but they're not green either. I wonder if they've changed since I first looked. Weird.

"Bye." He walks away. When he reaches the door, he says, "Hey, Caitlin."

"What?"

"I'll see you at school."

It takes me a second to realize he means *this* school. I laugh. "Oh . . . if I get in."

He laughs too. But he says, "You will. With a voice like that, you can do anything you want."

He's gone before I can say anything else. I look around. The room's cleared out, and I'm all alone. The sun's streaming through the dirty windows, and I watch Sean as he goes to the street. Then I watch his back until he is totally swallowed up by the glare.

𝄞 Opera_Grrrl's Online Journal

Subject: Hi!
Date: April 5
Time: 9:37 p.m.
Feeling: Thoughtful
Weight: 115 lbs. this morning (Eek!)
Days Since I Auditioned for Miami HS of the Arts: 23

Okay, so here's the deal. My former shrink, Lucia (*long* story), was after me 2 keep a journal. "Write your thoughts," she said. "U don't have 2 show anyone."

i.e, a pointless exercise. No thx! I do enough of those in SCHOOL!

Besides, who wants a notebook where anyone can read my "thoughts?" Like, what if I got hit by a bus??? I can just picture it: Mom, drumming her pink-manicured nails on my hosp. bed, all "Oh, sugar dumpling, I know u feel bad, but could u possibly explain this little thing on page 15?" Again: No thx!

But some of my friends started keeping these online journal things, & I thought that would be better. The anonymous thing is cool. The *world* can read it, but my ex-boyfriend, Internet stalkers, etc. ("etc." meaning my mother), won't know it's me. The journal name, Opera_Grrrl, is my secret identity. Think Clark Kent/Superman, Bruce Wayne/Batman.

Okay . . . . some important details:
Name: Well, I'm not going 2 tell you that (see above)
Age: 16
Occupation: Student @ a high school in Fla. (but thinking about making a change)
Hobbies/Interests: See above . . . . I love 2 sing!!!
Pet Peeves: People who think my hobbies & interests are weird
Dating Status: Unattached
The question ur all wondering about (even tho probably no 1 is reading this): The reason I had a therapist is b/c I recently broke up w/the boyfriend from HELL!!!

What is the Boyfriend from Hell? It is one who seems really perfect:
· wicked-hot
· nice car
· showed up on time
· brought flowers
· wrote poetry

But also:
· hit me
· told me I was fat
· said I should only hang out w/his friends b/c mine were all losers

· said no one would ever want 2 be w/me but him
· said my singing was stupid
· and, um, did I mention, HIT ME???

So this past Dec., I broke up w/him, & I actually went 2 court and got a piece of paper that says if he comes 2 close, I can call the cops & they will throw his butt in jail.

That's when I got the shrink. I went for a month or 2, sat in a circle w/other girls who'd had bad boyfriends, talked about them, wrote poetry about them, did interpretive dances about them, role-played what we'd say if we saw them, cried, etc., etc., etc . . . . then I got tired of wallowing in my problems so I stopped going. I use the time for practicing my singing now. *That's* therapy.

But every once in a while, I think about getting back together w/Nick. How wacko does that make me???

Which is why I'm also thinking about switching schools.

*E*x-boyfriend at 3:00. I fumble with my lock. He walks closer. I try not to look like I'm looking at him, but I also try not to look like I'm *not* looking at him, if that makes sense.

Of course it doesn't.

Ex-boyfriend at 2:30. I open my locker and stick my head completely inside. Maybe he won't notice me, and he'll just go away.

Yeah, right. He probably has my schedule tattooed on the back of his hand. Last month, I changed my locker *and* my lock because he broke in and left me flowers (white roses) for my birthday. It was beyond creepy.

I look around the side of my door. Ex-boyfriend at 1:00. Mayday! Mayday!

And . . . he's . . . past me.

I realize I haven't breathed in about a minute. I inhale quickly and exhale slowly, like I'm singing. I back away from my locker, all shaky. I can't even remember what I came here to get. I close it and stand, pretending to rest my hand against a locker. Really, I'm looking to see if Nick's still there, looking at me.

But he isn't looking. He's going around the corner. 9:00 . . . 8:00 . . .

Nick gets to the end of the hallway and turns. Our eyes meet a second. Then he looks away. I start walking in the opposite direction . . .

. . . and bump right into my friend Peyton.

"'Sup, girlfriend?" Peyton says.

I answer, truthfully, "I don't know." I hope she didn't see me looking at Nick.

No such luck. Peyton points to the corner Nick's just disappearing around. "Omigod, was that Nick? Were you talking to him, Cat?"

I wince at *Cat.* That's what Nick used to call me. My friends aren't known for their sensitivity, and I know Peyton's just looking for good gossip. Before Nick, I used to have real friends. But Nick made me dump them and just hang out with *his* friends, who were so fakey-perfect that staying friends with them was *work.* Now my old friends are mad at me for dumping them, and even though Nick's friends took my side in the breakup, I still don't know them that well—and they sure don't know me. If I cop to looking at him, it will be all over school by lunch.

I shake my head. "Are you on crack? No. No!"

She shakes her head. "Right. Sure. Of course not. So, you

going to the basketball pep rally, Friday?"

"Can't. There's a state competition for chorus in Tampa. We'll be there all day."

"God, I'd gouge my eyes out—missing important stuff for an *elective*. You should've taken driver's ed instead of chorus. Can't you just be sick that day?"

"I have a solo too." *One that I beat twelve other girls out for.*

Peyton rolls her eyes. "You would. Will you be back in time for the game?"

"I really, really hope so." *Not a snowflake's chance . . .*

"You know, you're not going to have time for that stuff if you make the squad next year. They expect you to be at every practice every game, unless you're, like, dead or something. And even then, you'd better have a note from the mortician."

Not a snowflake's chance of that either. I'm not trying out for cheerleading squad. I wouldn't make it anyway. I'm not what you'd call coordinated, and Peyton's right. I'd have to give up chorus. Which is so not happening. But I haven't figured out how to explain that to my friends. I know when I do, they'll ditch me for sure.

"Look," I say. "I've got to go to English. See you later."

"Caitlin?"

I want to look at my watch. But that would be rude, and I have to be nice or I won't have any friends at all. "What?"

"You're not getting back with Nick, are you?"

"Are you kidding? No. I wish I never had to even see him again."

I think that's true.

Subject: More about Nick
Date: April 7
Time: 4:01 p.m.
Feeling: Nervous
Weight: 116 lbs. this morning (Emergency!)
Days Since I Auditioned for Miami HS of the Arts: 25

No responses 2 my 1st entry, which proves no 1 is reading this. GOOD. I had this secret fear that every1 I ever met would magically figure out this was me!

Saw Nick in the hall 2day. He didn't say anything 2 me, which I guess is good. Maybe he's figured out that I'm not going 2 get back w/ him.

Two weeks ago, he called me and asked me 2 meet him @ the beach.

What I can't believe is: I didn't say no. I said yes. I was dressed & out the door b4 I came 2 my senses. But part of me maybe wanted 2 go.

Nick was the only guy I ever loved . . . . I liked him since 7th grade, only I wasn't hot enough 4 him 2 notice then. He's been part of my life always. And he was the only 1 I ever . . . . did anything with. It's hard 2 look at some1 you were so close 2 and say you're never going 2 speak 2 him again. The world is different w/out him. I dated this other guy 4 a while, but it wasn't the same.

After Nick & I broke up, even w/the restraining order, he followed me around, just far enough away that I'd look all paranoid if I said anything. I got hang-up calls 2. It wasn't his number on the Caller ID, but I knew it was him, maybe from a pay phone.

Sad Truth: It's flattering 2 think he still cares that much.

I feel him watching me in the halls. It's when I watch back that worries me.

ON 2 ANOTHER TOPIC . . . . I should be getting my letter from MHSA any day now . . . . I auditioned there almost a mo. ago & they said they'd get us the letters "next month." Next month means w/in 30 days, right? If they just meant sometime in April, I may die. OMGOMGOMG!

This makes me happy (I'm dying 2 find out if I got in!!!) but it worries me 2. Thing is I never told mom I was trying out b/c . . . .

· I wasnt sure if I wanted 2 go even if I do get in (I really might just want 2 know if I'm good enough)
· I'm not sure I'll get in & I don't even want her to know I tried out if I don't get in.

But she'll def. be mad I tried out w/out telling her, so I need 2 break the news gently if I get in.

So the way I've dealt w/this is . . . . I've been running home the moment the bell rings at 2:43 . . . .
. . . . actually SPRINTING home would be a better word 4 it (you'd think I'd be losing major poundage) . . . . knocking down unwary people in my path. Our mail gets delivered at 3

& mom's home then b/c she sells real estate . . . .
so I'm out there waiting for our pruny old mailman like I'm
hot 4 him . . . .

But on Fri. we have state chorus competition and I'll be
away when the mail comes. What if the letter comes
then????????

*T*he television isn't on when I get home. That's the first sign of a problem. There are always warning signs: Rattlesnakes rattle. Cats' fur stands on end. With my mother, the first sign of trouble is the eerie silence of a TV-free living room.

But maybe I'm just being crazy. The whole drive home from Tampa, I've been freaking out, not singing "Ninety-Nine Bottles of Beer on the Wall" with everyone else, not even whispering and giggling (okay, not *too* much) when Brianna Owens and Josh Eisenberg crawled up into the bus luggage rack and were definitely doing *way* more than just making out. Even then I was worried about Mom and the letter.

But what are the odds that the letter would have come today?

I stand by the door waiting for something to happen. It really is weird that the TV isn't on. There's always a makeover show on *some* station.

What are the odds?

Mom's sitting on the sofa, staring at something in her lap. I walk closer, talking. "Hey, we got a superior rating. I got a superior on my solo too, and . . ." I'm talking just enough so she won't comment on it when I leave.

She holds up the thing in her lap. It's a letter. *The* letter. I can see on the return address where it has the Miami High School of the Arts emblem thing.

Life lesson learned: Whenever you say, "What are the odds?" the odds-gods automatically up them to 100% certainty.

"What's this, Caitlin?"

I don't know. What is it? Acceptance or rejection? Acceptance or rejection?

"Um, I thought I'd try out for the performing arts school."

"You thought you'd try out? Don't you have to get a parent's permission to transfer to a new school?"

"Can I see the letter please?" I say, trying to be nice.

"When were you planning on telling me this? Or were you?"

"Of course I was going to tell you. I didn't transfer . . . I just wanted . . . Can I have the letter please? I want to see—"

She turns it over, and that's when I see for the first time that it's open. She read it! She read it before me. I'm trying really hard not to swallow my tongue.

"You opened it?"

"It was an accident. I thought it was junk mail."

"Opening other people's mail is a federal crime." I read that somewhere.

"I said it was an accident. Now answer my question."

"Give me my letter!"

"Caitlin!"

"Give me my letter!"

I'm sure I didn't get in, and the thought of Mom knowing that just kills me. Up until now, I'd been telling myself that I wasn't sure I wanted to go, that maybe I wanted to stay at Key Biscayne High with my friends. But now I know that's a lie. If someone gave me a choice between an acceptance and *breathing* for the next five minutes . . . well, I'd have to think about it.

"Give me my letter!" With each time I yell it, I get louder until she's holding her ears.

"Caitlin, stop yelling. I have the windows open. The neighbors—"

"Then give it to me! It's mine!"

"Caitlin, how could you do something like this . . . try to switch schools without telling me?"

"Would you stop making it about you? It's not always about you!"

"I'm your mother. I'm practically the only parent you have, and I—"

Her voice fades to static because that's when I figure it out. I got in. If it was a rejection, she wouldn't be mad. She'd be all sweetie and honey, comforting poor Caitlin who'd failed. Again. Don't worry, sugarplum, Mommy's here to pick up the pieces of your broken heart, as the old song goes. But if she's mad, it could only mean . . .

I grab the letter. I'm giggling and crying, and I grab the letter from her and run until I get to the bedroom. I slam the door and lock it.

Dear Caitlin: We are pleased . . .

The letters swim before me, and I read it over and over again, memorizing it:

Dearcaitlinwearepleasedtoinviteyoutobepartoftheclassof . . . and I'm jumping up and down, screaming and smiling so hard I feel like my face might explode out of my throat. Mom's pounding on the door, and I'm dancing and screaming, "I got in!" at the same time she's screaming, "You're not going!"

♪ Opera_Grrrl's Online Journal

Subject: Miami HS of the Arts Letter
Date: April 11
Time: 9:37 p.m.
Listening 2: Mad Scene from Lucia di Lammermoor
(which mom hates b/c it's 2 screechy)
Feeling: Crazed
Weight: 115 lbs. this morning

Guess what came 2day?
The good news: got in.
The bad news: can't go.

I stop typing and eat three gummy bears—green, yellow, and red. My jeans feel tighter when I do this, though gummies only have nine calories each (times three). The thing about losing a lot of weight is that it feels temporary, like you're just a *thin* fatgirl, and one good Big Mac will send you exploding from your jeans again. I weighed a hundred and five when I left camp last year. Since then I've gained and lost the same fifteen pounds a dozen times. Right now, I weigh one-fifteen, which is what the weight charts say you're supposed to weigh at five-three. The guy who made the weight chart (and I'm sure it was a guy) didn't go to my school, though. At my school, the most you can weigh is one-ten, even if you're five-foot-nine.

I toss the rest of the bag into the wastebasket, stare at the computer screen, and listen to the opera on CD. This is the part where the soprano just went completely nuts and stabbed a guy. She's covered in blood, singing like crazy in her nightgown in front of a crowd of people . . . all because her family wouldn't just let her do what she wanted to do.

I can *sooooo* relate.

I wake to the sound of screaming.

"Lance! Are you aware of the date?"

My mother. I check the clock on the night table. Seven-thirty.

"It's April twelfth. Twelve! That's eleven days late for this month, and we still don't have March!"

Ah. Daddy-kins is late on the child support. Again.

"If I don't get that check, I'll have to buy her clothes at Wal-Mart! Do you care?"

I really don't think my dad cares where she buys my clothes. I think about the gummies in the garbage.

"*You* try and feed and clothe a sixteen-year-old on what you give me! The least you could do is not insult us by being late on top of everything. *Really* late."

I take the bag from the garbage, then go to the bathroom, and shake the bears into the toilet. They scream as they whirl down the drain. I read once that Lindsay Lohan, the actress, dumps her Diet

Coke onto her plate when she's through eating so she won't be tempted to graze, which is why you can see every bone in her neck like it's on display. I need to do that. Closer to the bedroom, Mom's voice is louder.

"No, I don't use the money for myself. We had an agreement, Lance! Lance! Don't you dare hold the phone away from your ear!"

I'm about to turn the stereo louder, the better to avoid Mom's Vengeance Aria, when I hear the finale.

"You think you could do better, raising her?" She laughs. "I'd like to see that!"

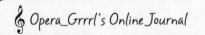 Opera_Grrrl's Online Journal

Subject: In Their Gummy Graves
Date: April 12
Time: 8:00 a.m.
Feeling: Determined

Miami HS of the Arts Possibilities

· Work on Mom
· Forge Mom's signature on registration paperwork
· Stay at Key Biscayne High, be a cheer-girl & get stalked by ex
· Try 2 live with Dad???

I hit the backspace button and erase the last one.

The first thing I remember my father doing was leaving. That was the second thing too, and the third, and the tenth. My father was always leaving for something—business trips, double-secret golf weekends. Then one day when I was five, he got tired of coming home for fresh Jockey shorts and he left for good.

The day he left, in a scene reminiscent of *The Parent Trap* but without the British accents, my parents divided up the important stuff: Mom got me. Dad got the Porsche. I can still see myself wearing my favorite *Sleeping Beauty* dress (I loved Aurora because she looked just like Mom). We came home from preschool, and Dad was loading his suitcase into the trunk of the aforementioned Porsche. I asked if he was going on a trip. He looked at Mom.

She shrugged, like, "You tell her," and he said no, he was leaving for good.

Note word choice: For good. He didn't say what I now know are the usual meaningless things about how we'd still be a family, that it wasn't my fault. He said he was leaving for good. I had no idea what "for good" meant, except it didn't sound any good to me. I started crying. He yelled at Mom that she brought me home on purpose to make it hard for him and that this was the kind of crap she always did. Finally, he pried my fat fingers from his pants leg and drove away.

Mom held me, to keep me from being crushed by the

Porsche, then said, "We should have dinner at Mickey D's. A shake always helps."

"No!" I didn't want a shake. I wanted everything to go back to the screwed-up way it was. Finally, I agreed to go. I got a shake. A Shamrock, because it was March. Large. Since then mint ice cream has always made me sick. It's one thing I can't eat. But if I had to guess, I'd guess that's also the day I started eating when I felt bad.

Some people fantasize about their dads coming back, or about going to live with them. Not me! I see Dad twice a year, at Thanksgiving *or* Christmas (not both, even though he only lives twenty minutes away), and again on Easter. For a long time, I associated Dad with the smell of sweet potatoes. Mom drives me to his place, which he shares with his lovely wife, Macy, and their charming daughters, Thing One and Thing Two. I get there an hour before dinner and leave an hour after. I always get presents, even on Thanksgiving, since Macy wraps my Christmas gifts early. Last Easter, the bunny brought me a Movado watch, all stuffed inside a pink plastic egg. I spent the next week trying to figure out how to convert it to cash. The stupid thing would've paid for an opera subscription or a lifetime supply of sheet music. But the jeweler would only give merchandise credit.

So I don't kid myself about Dad. Even if Mom hasn't exactly been supportive—even if she's sort of a witch—she is, as she constantly reminds me, my only parent. I know that. That's why it's unfair of me to think about asking Dad to move in with him, just for a few months, until Mom realizes that Miami High School of the Arts is a good idea.

It's also completely stupid, because I know he'd never take me.

*A*ll weekend, the letter sits on my bed. I pick it up every few hours, just to look at it, like I used to do with the ring Nick gave me, before I gave it back.

I avoid Mom. I stay in my room, watch television, and eat there too. She thinks she won our argument, but I'm not giving in that quickly. And I listen to music, *loud* music, opera music I know she hates, like the Queen of the Night's Vengeance Aria, which has four high Fs in about two minutes. I listen to that over and over. But Mom's working most of the weekend, so she's out. It's no fun not speaking to someone if they don't even know you're not speaking to them.

But Sunday morning, we collide in the kitchen.

My mother sells real estate, or she tries to. She also sells Emma Leigh cosmetics—that company that awards its top sellers a purple Mustang convertible. Mom got one of those a few years ago—the high point of her existence (we had a party with purple streamers and purple foods, even the meat). Mom didn't work right after Dad left. She just sat in this house, doing her nails, waiting for Dad's monthly alimony checks. Then I guess Dad wised up, so she had to get a job. Or rather, she got her real estate license *and* started selling Emma Leigh. She's out of the house a lot now, which is great, but she must not sell much, considering she's still completely on the dole from Dad. Once, years ago, I opened one of his monthly checks, and I almost fell over at the amount. Dad might as well be one of those guys in Utah with two wives.

Anyway, the kitchen. Today's Sunday. Mom has open houses most Sundays, so after I hear the garage door go down, I head for the kitchen, planning to sit there for the approximately nineteen seconds it takes to consume my lunchbox-sized, fat-, sugar-, and taste-free key lime yogurt (90 calories). I open the fridge.

When I close it, she's there.

"Oh!" I say, forgetting I'm not speaking to her. "Thought you left."

She's carrying a pink plastic lawn flamingo she named Harold and dresses in little costumes: a ghost on Halloween, a leprechaun on St. Patrick's Day, which is how it's dressed right now. "I went to change Harold into his Easter bonnet. Want to help?"

For this chore, she has on a blue crop top that manages to show off both her boobs *and* her (pierced) belly button, denim butt shorts, and cherry red platforms. Mom is thirty-seven, but she looks twenty-five and dresses like thirteen. She tried to get me to call her Val in public, so people wouldn't know she was my mother. But I said that would just be too alternative universe.

"No, that's okay."

"You always used to help me with Harold."

Yeah, I thought it was cute when I was, like, seven. I remember I'm not speaking to her and turn and head for the table, so she'll remember too.

But she puts Harold down and follows me. I sit, and she's behind me, touching my hair, acting like Friday never happened. "Time for a little trim!"

"I got my hair cut last month." Then I add, "The day before auditions." You know, just to remind her.

She ignores that, running her hands through my hair. I know her nails are blue without even looking.

Sheesh—why'd I have to look?

"I know," she says, "but how about something different this time. Like layers."

Something different being secret code for, *I really hate the way it looks now.*

When Mom and I can't talk about anything else, we talk about beauty products. Beauty products mean something to Mom. She thinks if I'd just take her advice on beauty and fashion, my life would be better. I used to think so too, but now I think it would be better if she left me alone.

"I don't want layers," I say. "You talked me into layers once, and they made me look like a marigold."

"*Long* layers. And we can go together and get our nails done. It'll be fun."

Fun for her because whenever we go out together, all the sales-people and hairdressers crowd around, talking about how we look like sisters. "No, thanks."

Mom was a great beauty in college. She was homecoming princess her freshman year, and rode down the street on a float, waving. I'm sure Mom would have come back the next year and been queen.

But by the next year, she'd managed to hook Dad, and she dropped out of college, anyway, so she never made it to queen.

When I was a homecoming princess last year at school, she said, "Maybe you'll be queen next year," even though the best you can be is a princess, unless you're a senior. She couldn't just be happy about that.

"I like my hair the way it is now," I say.

"Sometimes a person needs a change."

"I know. That's why I want to go to Miami High School of the Arts."

"Caitlin, that school is in a bad neighborhood in downtown Miami."

Translation: She's afraid there'll be black kids there.

"I'm trying to protect you. I wouldn't feel right sending a sixteen-year-old there."

Translation: It will inconvenience her.

"The other kids are sixteen too. Some are fifteen."

I wait for her to say I'm a *young* sixteen, which translates to, *If I'm pretending to be twenty-five, you can't possibly be sixteen.* Wait for it.

"Yes, but you're a *young* sixteen, Caitlin. You've been sheltered and haven't always had the best judgment."

"Sheltered?" But I know the translation for that too.

"You're going to throw Nick in my face forever, aren't you?" I say.

"I'm not throwing anything in your face. I haven't said anything about that . . . boy for months. But I do wish we could talk about it. You're always so secretive. I didn't even know you were dating someone else."

"Who said I am?"

"Shelley Silverberg said she saw you in a car with some boy in a football jersey."

Why do grown-ups always call guys "boys"? "It wasn't Nick. God, why do you always have to assume—?"

"Because we don't talk. That's why I thought it would be fun to spend a day together, catch up on things. I don't know anything about your life, Caitlin."

"I don't want to talk to you about guys. The only thing in my life that's important is the only thing you don't want to talk about—singing. That's my life."

"You're in chorus at school. But I don't see why you should put yourself at risk, going downtown."

"Because I'm serious about singing. I want to do it for a living."

She sighs. "Singing isn't a practical career choice, Caitlin. How will you support yourself?"

"By singing. It's what I'm good at."

"Maybe it's time to forget chorus and concentrate on your studies."

I want to ask her why? *Why?* So I'll end up in my thirties, collecting child support like her? No thanks. I want to do something with my life.

"I guess if it doesn't work out, I can always sell makeup," is what I manage.

I turn and scrape my yogurt cup. It takes everything I have not to turn around, not to do the usual Caitlin thing and try to smooth things over, say I didn't mean it.

I did mean it, and some things shouldn't be smoothed over.

We stand there a full minute, and I wait for her to leave. But instead, she strokes my hair. "Long layers, Caitlin. Think how pretty it could be."

♪ Opera_Grrrl's Online Journal

Subject: Ryan Seacrest is my life raft!
Date: April 19
Time: 7:40 a.m.
Listening 2: American Top 40
Feeling: Determined

I am sitting, listening 2 AT40. None of my friends know I do this, but every Sunday morning, I sit for 4 WHOLE HOURS and cram so I can know which songs are popular (inc. the

---

artists' names) . . . . instead of which songs were popular in 1850!

Problem: I *hate* the Top 40. I don't even know how they got 2 *be* the Top 40. Even the type of music they play on the University of Miami station would be better, but that's not what average kids listen 2. And I want 2 be average.

I just *know* if I went 2 Miami HS of the Arts, I wouldn't have 2 do this anymore! I could actually *admit* 2 liking opera. I could admit 2 not being average.

*D*ude!" Ashley stares at my Wendy's taco salad as if it just sprouted legs and started to walk off its Styrofoam bed. "You're not actually going to eat that?"

It's Sunday, a week after I got my letter. I still haven't told anyone but Mom (since that went so well). Dealing with her parentnoia is more than enough without having to endure the Seven Stages of Grief from my friends.

"Um, I was thinking about it," I say. Seems like a strange question, considering I ordered and now *own* said taco salad. "I mean, why not? It's a salad."

"It's a taco salad," Peyton says, like that explains everything.

"So?" I'm missing something here, some Rosetta Stone that will translate what they're saying into English. I'm guessing I ordered the wrong thing.

When I used to see Peyton and Ashley around school, I couldn't tell them apart. Now that we've been friends almost a year, it's still hard—identical flat stomachs in crop tops (but

Ashley's top is plain, while Peyton's says CHEERLEADERS ARE ATHLETES TOO!), identical noses (though I now know that Peyton's is real, while Ashley brought a photo of Peyton to the plastic surgeon who corrected her deviated septum), wardrobes, fake Southern accents, and not-quite-identical streaked hair (Ashley's is redder). Only by spending an insane amount of time with them do you see a difference: Peyton's mostly harmless. Ashley's potentially lethal.

But they're my friends. When the whole ugly Nick thing happened, I thought they'd take his side since they were really his friends to begin with, and leave me with no one. So when Peyton and Ashley stuck by me, I was grateful. Confused, but grateful.

"So it's . . . never mind, Cat. It looks yummy." Ashley hands me a packet of sour cream that came with the salad. "Wouldn't want to forget this."

I lift my plastic fork, and Peyton yelps, like she might throw herself on the salad to save me from it. "She means it's a salad with six hundred seventy calories—two hundred ninety from fat—thirty-two fat grams and eighty-five carbohydrate grams *with* the sour cream. Without it . . ."

She keeps going. I tune out, listening to the elevator music version of a Kelly Clarkson song and trying to remember if Peyton was the one who failed business math.

"If you eat that," she finishes, "you can't eat anything else the rest of the day!"

I think about the bagel and cream cheese I had only two hours ago and wave off the sour cream Ashley's holding out. "Too fattening."

"You only lose fifty calories and three and a half fat grams by not having sour cream," Peyton says. "But you lose two hundred and ten calories, nine fat grams, and twenty-nine carb grams if you leave off the chips."

But then what would be the point of having a taco salad?

Ashley squeezes half of her packet of fat-free French dressing onto her spring mix salad (I bet Peyton knows the numbers on that one too), and says, "Oh, leave her alone, Pey. Let her eat whatever she wants." She glances at my thighs, then her own skeletal ones. "I need to lose ten pounds. I'm so fat."

"You're so not," I say. She knows she isn't, but smiles. It's a game they play, the *I'm so fat* game, which you can only play it if you've never been a fatgirl in your life. I leave the chips and pick at the lettuce. I lift my legs so my thighs won't sploosh out on the plastic seat. "I wish I had your thighs," I add, and Ashley nods, all happy.

"I went shopping yesterday . . ." Peyton rolls her eyes. "With my mom."

"Mallicide!" Ashley clutches Peyton's arm.

"Did she at least buy you anything good?" I ask, knowing how her brain works.

"Negatory. It's really hard for me to find anything, what with my size and all. I wear a zero, and hardly anything comes in that, only Rampage and a few others."

"Rampage is nice," I say.

Peyton and Ashley exchange looks.

I've said the wrong thing. I try again. "How about Express?"

"Too big."

"Wet Seal?"

"Huge."

"The Gap, Banana Republic, Old Navy?" I've bought clothes at all these stores since I got thin. But I've never been as thin as Peyton and Ashley.

"Too big, too big, too big *and* too cheap. Hell-o? Old Navy's, like, the cheap version of the Gap."

I look at Ashley, who nods, confirming that this is, indeed, the sad case, and adjusts her top. I just read an article that said the crop top is out. Obviously, that was written by some hopeful fat-girl because all my friends are still wearing them.

"So, what are you wearing to cheerleader tryouts next week?" Peyton asks.

"Um, I'm not sure I can go," I say, bracing for the nuclear reaction this will cause.

Total shocksville.

"But why?" Ashley asks.

"I don't know." I toy with my salad fork and think. "I'm just not athletic like you guys. I'll look stupid. And I'm not sure I want to be a cheerleader."

"But it's cheerleading! *Everyone* wants to be a cheerleader."

"Caitlin doesn't want what everyone wants," Peyton says,

pushing aside her half-eaten salad.

"Well, what *do* you want?"

I have a flash of memory, like a digital photo the second after the snap, of Sean Griffin's face. I wonder what it would be like to have friends—or even a boyfriend—who actually *get* me, people who don't think opera and Oprah are the same thing. I squeeze the sour cream packet onto my salad, trying to figure out how to explain it to them without seeming snobby.

I can't. I change the subject. "Did you hear about Brianna Owens and Josh Eisenberg in the luggage compartment of the bus, coming back from the chorus trip?"

"No!" Ashley says. "That skank!"

And the subject is changed. I pour out all the details I remember, considering I wasn't paying attention, and they jabber about how could anyone want Josh Eisenberg's *anything* in her mouth, and I relax. They're happy if they're trashing someone . . . Do they trash me if I'm not there? Probably. Doesn't matter. While they're doing that, I'm free to think about other things. It's been happening more and more lately.

I pick at my taco salad and think Maria Callas, a diva who— this is probably urban legend—sometimes went on a raw-meat diet, because it gave her tapeworms, parasites that helped her lose weight. Yuck. But I understand.

I'm in the middle of that thought when I hear a voice across the restaurant.

"Caitlin!"

I ignore it, thinking it must be some other Caitlin, but it comes closer.

"Caitlin!" I turn then and see Sean Griffin walking toward us holding a taco salad identical to my own and a cup of water. "I'm right, right? It's Caitlin?"

I've lost the ability to speak. I nod. Are my friends staring?

"Mind if I sit?" He does so, in the empty seat by mine. He opens his salad and starts squeezing sour cream onto it. I watch him. He's wearing loose khakis and a yellow-and-white-striped button-down, which look like they've been washed a hundred times. The shirt has a tiny hole under the collar, but the pants are ironed to a crease. *He's poor*, I think, trying the thought on for size. I've never known anyone poor. Actually, *I've* always been the poorest of my friends, with their massive allowances, houses straight out of *MTV Cribs*, and vacation places in Marco Island and the Keys.

I can see his skin through that little hole, and I lean closer, fixated on it, almost wanting to reach out with the tip of my finger and touch it . . . him.

I draw back, realizing he's watching me. In his loose clothes, he looks skinnier than in the unitard. Maybe I'm just seeing him through Peyton and Ashley's eyes.

Introduce him to your friends before he thinks you're stupid.

Probably too late.

"Peyton Berounski and Ashley Pettigrew, this is Sean. Sean Griffin."

He takes them in, top to bottom. I can actually see his thoughts, like subtitles on televised operas—*Sheesh, cheerleaders!* I almost laugh. But then he smiles. "Hey, great to meet you." He turns back to me. "So? You got in, right?"

I force a smile. "Um, yeah. I mean, sort of. Not really. I mean, yeah, I got in, but I didn't. I mean, I'm not going."

Sean yells, "Not going?" at the same time Peyton and Ashley start in with, "Got in where? Not going where?"

"Nothing. It's not important. I mean, I tried out for Miami High School of the Arts, just to see if I'd get in, and I decided I'd rather stay at Key with all my friends than transfer junior year." I can't look at Sean. "So you live around here?"

"No, I work at a church near here. Don't change the subject. What do you mean, you're not going?" To Peyton and Ashley, he says, "Your friend's a fabulous singer—she's going to be the next Renée Fleming."

Like they know who she is. "Thanks. I don't . . . I just didn't think it was for me."

"Of course, it isn't," Ashley says. "That's where all the goths go."

"And the freaks," Peyton adds. "I see them on the train when we go downtown for Heat games. They don't get out of school until, like, four-thirty, and they're all there, singing and dancing on the Metrorail platform." She wrinkles her nose. "So weird."

I still can't look at Sean, so I sit there, picturing a girl I once saw, doing what Peyton's talking about; a girl in a black leotard with long, black hair, stretching and dancing between the columns, and none of her friends acted like that was weird at all. I watched her, even as the train pulled away, thinking she looked like a bat, dark and beautiful against the brilliant Miami skyline. I wanted to be her.

"I'm sorry you won't be there," I hear Sean say.

"Yeah," Ashley says. "It's a shame. Well, it was nice meeting you. Gotta go."

I follow them, because that's what I've become: a follower.

They're barely outside before they start trashing him.

"Your friend's going to be the next Brunhilde Fatso," Ashley mimics.

"'She's fabulous!'" Peyton giggles. "He talks like you, Cait, all opera-y."

My friends don't get the opera thing. To them, it's all fat ladies with horns, and I don't even try to explain it. When I was a lonely fatgirl, I always had opera. Now I have other things, so I should give it up. But I don't want to. I want to run to that school; maybe it's running for my life.

"What was up with his shirt?" Peyton says. "It had a hole in it."

"You should've given him your chips," Ashley says. "He was so scrawny."

"Like you'd want to go to that freaky school. Why'd you even try out?"

We reach Ashley's car. I put my hand on it, steadying myself, feeling the warmth against my hand. I look through the window and see Sean looking at me. "I just wanted to see if I'd get in, okay? But I'm not going. My mom would never let me."

I hold my breath. They hate my mom, even though they're a lot like her. But Ashley says, "Yeah, well, even your mom can be right once in a while."

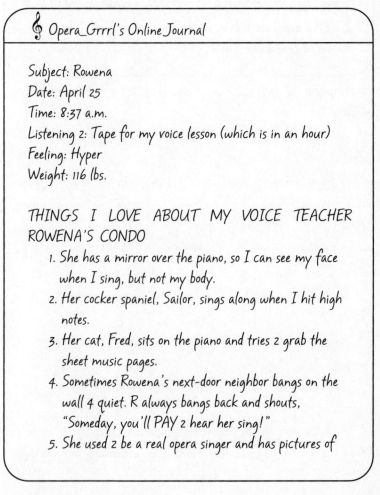

🎼 Opera_Grrrl's Online Journal

Subject: Rowena
Date: April 25
Time: 8:37 a.m.
Listening 2: Tape for my voice lesson (which is in an hour)
Feeling: Hyper
Weight: 116 lbs.

THINGS I LOVE ABOUT MY VOICE TEACHER ROWENA'S CONDO

1. She has a mirror over the piano, so I can see my face when I sing, but not my body.
2. Her cocker spaniel, Sailor, sings along when I hit high notes.
3. Her cat, Fred, sits on the piano and tries 2 grab the sheet music pages.
4. Sometimes Rowena's next-door neighbor bangs on the wall 4 quiet. R always bangs back and shouts, "Someday, you'll PAY 2 hear her sing!"
5. She used 2 be a real opera singer and has pictures of

herself playing Suzuki in Madame Butterfly at the NYC Opera!!!
6. Rowena thinks I'm special and talented.

So why am I lying 2 Rowena??? It's been 2 weeks since I got the letter from MHSA . . . . Every week, she asks me if I got it & every week I say no. It's just . . . . she'll be so disappointed that I can't go.

$\mathcal{M}$y voice lesson's almost over, and she hasn't asked me yet. Maybe I'll get out without lying today. Rowena stops playing the piano. "So, have you heard?"

Or not. "Um, nope. Nothing yet."

She grins. "Good. Then I get to tell you. I talked to a friend of mine who teaches at the school. You got in!"

"Great. Wow . . . um . . . that's great."

"Isn't it? They're all so excited about having you there."

"Great." *Do you know another word?* "Wonderful . . ."

"What's wrong, Caitlin?"

At this point, Fred the cat nuzzles my shoulder, and I mumble, "I'm not sure I want to. I mean, I'm really happy studying with you. I don't want anything to change."

This is something I've thought about. I've been taking voice with Rowena since middle school. I had to beg Dad to pay for lessons, and I had to ride my bike to get there (still do), but it's worth it. Rowena used to be a real opera singer. She traveled all over the world, but gave it up to raise her kids. The coolest thing about Rowena is she's nothing like my mom. She's like the Anti-Mom. She's let her hair go gray and she wears it long down her back, and probably doesn't even *own* any makeup. Rowena knows just how much to push me—enough so I have something to work for, but not so much that I want to drink gasoline after a lesson. And she'd never tell me to get long layers.

I'd miss it a lot if I couldn't study with her, and maybe I wouldn't have time if I changed schools.

But she says, "That's the coolest part though. I just got a job there myself."

"You what?"

"Yeah, I thought now that Harmony's in college, I could work full-time. If you go, I can see you every day. Isn't that just cool?"

I agree it's very, very cool, even though my head's pounding now, but her voice is all excited, and she asks again if I'm going to go. I hear myself say, "Sure."

She wipes her hand across her forehead like, Whew! What a relief! "That's so great. I was worried because, with the new job, I probably won't have much time for my private students. But this way, I can keep you on."

"You mean you couldn't otherwise?" *Because, um, my head's about to explode.*

"It doesn't really matter now, does it, since you're going?"

"No." I agree that no, it doesn't matter, and yes, it's really wonderful, and then I ask if we can sing some more, because I really want to work on this piece I'm doing. It goes up to a high E-flat, and that's the closest I can get to socially acceptable screaming.

𝄞 Opera_Grrrl's Online Journal

Subject: I am *Such* a Liar
Date: April 25
Time: 11:03 p.m.
Listening 2: Medea
Feeling: Worried
Weight: Same

   I'm listening 2 Medea (see above). It's abt. this wicked sorceress from Greek myths. Right now, Medea's singing about how much she hates her ex-husband, Jason, how much she loves their kids, and finally—hey—why not kill the 2nd 2 get revenge on the 1st?
   In her room, Mom's screaming @ Dad about child support—now almost a month late.
   See the irony???

I stop typing and turn off the stereo. A few minutes ago, Mom came in and said it was almost eleven and she had a headache, and couldn't I just listen to rap music or something like other kids. I left it on until now just to prove my point.

"Do you want to go to court?" Mom screeches. Then she sings an aria about what her lawyer will do to Dad if that happens.

A pause while Dad checks his bank balance.

Then I guess he says something because she yells, "Oh, I'd like to see that!"

And she hangs up.

Mom's in the bathroom when I walk in. She has all her Emma Leigh products in front of her on the counter. When I was little, she used to let me put makeup on her, like she was a big, pretty doll. She'd do makeovers on me too, and tell me that someday, when I lost weight (she called it "baby fat"), I'd be so pretty . . . just like her. Everyone would want to date me. I once went to career day dressed as a cosmetologist.

She hasn't offered to do my makeup since I got thin and might actually look good.

I say, "What would you like to see?"

She jumps. "Oh . . . Caitlin . . . thought you were sleeping. The noi— singing stopped."

"You told me to stop. What were you telling Dad you'd like to see?"

She sighs. "Caitlin, when you get to be my age, you'll understand that sometimes, just occasionally, a person needs quiet."

"I understand," I say. "Really."

"I hope so."

"So what'd Dad say?"

"Dad?" She tries to look like she doesn't know what I'm talking about. It doesn't work. I notice a book on her dressing table. *Find a Husband After 35.* Terrific.

"You don't scream at anyone else like that," I say.

She slathers makeup remover on one eyelid, then dabs at it with a tissue. "I wasn't screaming." I give her a *yeah, right* look. "Well, he just makes me so mad. He thinks he can just do . . . whatever, the usual stuff. His kids—his *other* kids are in private school that costs as much as a Honda Accord—*per year, per kid,* but he thinks I should sell this house and move us to the middle of the stinkin' Everglades if I need money."

Sounds like Dad. He can definitely afford the child support, but I'm guessing he hates having his ex-wife and ex-kid sucking money out of him that he'd rather spend, buying out the entire stock of Limiteds One and Too, for Macy and the girls. I can't imagine not living in this house. We've been here forever. The way I see it, Dad owes me that money—he doesn't give me anything else.

"Yeah, he's a jerk," I say and mean it. We share a rare moment of mother-daughter solidarity. *One, two, three . . .*

"That's why you need to be careful, Caitlin. Once you have kids with someone, you're stuck with them forever." She tosses out the mascara-blackened tissue and starts on the rest of her face with Emma Leigh makeup remover.

Love you too, Mommy.

"I mean stuck with the man, not the kids."

"Sure." I try again. "What did you mean when you said you'd like to see that?"

She moves her fingers in circles along her cheekbones. "Hmm? Oh, he threatened to try and get custody if I kept nagging for money. As if."

She likes to do that, use expressions she thinks sound youthful. But she's always behind, so by the time she discovers something, no one's saying it except people on TV. "You really should have a beauty routine, Cait. Moisturizer and night cream. Young people think they're invincible, but once those crow's-feet show up, it's too late."

"There's always Botox." I'm still processing the idea—me living with Dad. Obviously, he didn't mean it, not unless Macy needs a free babysitter. But maybe . . . "Mom, I really want to go to Miami High School of the Arts."

"Caitlin, we've been over this."

"No, actually, we haven't. You just said no, that it isn't safe."

I know I could get her to let me go in a second, just by saying I want to get away from Nick. She'd have to let me go then. She went with me for the restraining order. But I hate to play that card. It makes me seem too pathetic.

"I still think so," she says.

"Rowena has a job teaching there. She says we could probably take the train together." Rowena didn't say that. But Mom doesn't know. I try not to notice her nose getting all wrinkly when I mention Rowena's name.

"Caitlin . . ." She finishes removing her makeup and tosses the last greasy tissue into the toilet. I watch it floating, making a film on the water. I think of Rowena, gone, and me, trapped here with Peyton and Ashley; trapped in this cheerless cheer-girl existence, when really, I want to be like that girl at the train station.

Mom's rinsing her face, and when she turns off the water, I hand her a towel.

"You know," I say, "if I moved in with Dad, I bet he'd let me go."

I'm here. Now what?

107 lbs. I've been Slim-Fasting for two weeks to make a good first impression. I feel a little light-headed.

Everyone here's like Peyton and Ashley said, and they all seem to know one another—maybe they've been having secret meetings all summer.

Right, Caitlin.

At the front of the room, an African-American girl with great cornrows is playing the piano. A guy is standing beside her, improvising a song about . . .

"I looooove your armpits! They are so fiiiiiiiine!"

Yup. Armpits. Check.

"Hey, Diva!"

I turn.

"Yeah, you. You're the one that sang *Phantom* at auditions, right? You made it."

Now, I recognize her by her voice. It's Eyebrow-Ring Girl. But now her hair's bright white and very short. She notices me staring.

"Are you, like, so shocked?"

"Oh." I laugh. "It's . . . pretty."

"Pretty weird. My mom stopped looking freaked by the red, so I tried this."

"When I'm away from your arrrrmpits, nothing is the same!"

She runs a hand across her hair. "Was that your mom who dropped you off?"

I sort of sigh without meaning to. Mom had to drop me off today (other days, I'll take the train, thank God) and wore one of her "business" outfits—a red miniskirted suit with a matching lace cami. In case *I* wasn't weird enough.

"Probably wouldn't take much to shock her," the girl says.

"What's that mean?" I snap.

"Sorry." The girl puts her hands in front of her, protectively. She gazes at me a minute, then asks, "Do you do pageants?"

"Huh? Of course not." But I feel my homecoming princess banner like a piece of skin across my chest. *How did she peg me so easily? Does she remember my dress from auditions* (I did better today—standard issue capri jeans and a blue T-shirt—but I still manage to look overdressed compared to most people). I'm too weird for the cheerleader crowd and too cheerleader for the weird crowd.

"I want your armpits today, and I'll still want them tomorrow."

"Oh, I just thought I recognized you from somewhere. I'm Gigi. I used to do pageants as a kid. Then my parents got divorced, and my mom moved here because it's a better pageant state. Last year, she made me enter Miss Teen Miami."

"Wow. Did you win?" I size her up like Mom would. She's skinny and pretty, but doesn't have the hair to be a pageant type.

"What do you think?" She raises an eyebrow. "I didn't exactly try my hardest. I might have slightly—and I mean just *slightly*—let some of my butt hang out of my bathing suit."

"On purpose?"

"You bet. You're supposed to spray your butt with glue so the suit won't ride up. But Mom was all, 'We'll show 'em next time.' So I killed her dreams with this." She gestures to the eyebrow-ring, which I now see is shaped like a little crown. "I told her it made me feel better about losing. She wasn't real sympathetic. But you looked like the type who'd go in for stuff like that."

"If I can't have your armpits, then let me have your loooooooove!"

"Well, I'm not." The music wails in my ears, and Gigi's talking, and it's just too much. I get up. "Excuse me."

Terrific. Making enemies already. The song finishes, and everyone looks when I stand. It's 7:28 and already I know this was a huge, huge mistake. Is it too late to register at my old school? I walk down the steps to the group clustered around the piano. The armpit guy is finished, and the girl who was playing piano starts in on an equally gross song about nose hair. I'm blown away that people can improvise like this when all I can do is sing other people's music.

No, it's easy. Just think of something gross. *Boogers.*

Boogers, boogers are so sweet. They are things I like to eat.

I can *not* sing that!

"Caitlin, you made it!"

I'm not surprised to see Sean Griffin. Actually, I realize I've been looking for him the whole time. He's with a girl I've never seen before.

"Yeah," I say. "My mom changed her mind."

Actually, Mom accused me of blackmail, but I didn't care. I had to go. I felt like I used to feel when I was a fatgirl, outgrowing all my clothes, like I might blow up.

So I told her if I couldn't come here, I'd move in with Dad. I lied. I *knew* she'd never let that happen, never let her nice, easy ride disappear.

"That's great." He gestures toward the girl. Actually, now that I look, she's clinging to him like a barnacle. "Caitlin, this is Misty."

Misty doesn't smile. She's this fattish blonde in a low-cut, tight pink crop top. She doesn't really look at me, because that would mean taking her eyes off of Sean. "Come on, Shawnee. Octavio saved us seats."

"See you around." Sean follows her to the empty seats which are—apparently—near everyone they've ever met in their lives. I look around for an empty seat, but the only one left without someone in it is the one I left. By Gigi.

She smiles and glances at Sean. "Nice."

"I guess so. I wasn't really planning on thinking about . . . guys this year. I want to get serious about singing."

That's true, isn't it?

"Probably for the best. Most guys here are gay."

I look at Sean and Barnacle Girl, still barnacling. "Obviously not him."

The nose hair song's still going. Gigi says, "You *are* serious."

"What?"

"You said you wanted to get serious about singing. You're plenty serious."

"How do you know?"

"Because I *heard* you. You're good. You're better than most people here."

Is she for real? "Yeah, I thought you were incredible too. Everyone here's really talented."

She shrugs. "Not everyone. But it definitely beats regular school."

I nod. "I lied to people at my old school—told them I was moving in with my Dad, so I wouldn't have to explain that I just wanted to get away from them."

"Running screaming from conformity," she says.

"Yeah. Something like that."

But even though I'd lied about moving in with Dad, Ashley'd figured out the real reason—that I was going to performing arts school. "You'll be back," she'd said. "You might think you're weird enough to hang with those people, but you're not." I wonder if she's right.

A woman who must be the Drama teacher shows up. She's sixty-something, short, with hair that auburn color older people get that almost looks purplish, a flowing green shirt and pants, and the highest heels I've ever seen. She stands front and center, glaring, until everyone's silent.

"Welcome to the theater," she says, "to the magic. To the fun."

I wonder if that's from a play or if she just talks like that. A few people laugh.

She continues. "I'm Miss Lorraine Davis. I want to be *called* Miss Davis. I'll be your Drama teacher on this fabulous ride you call high school. As musical theater majors, you should know that acting is as important as singing. I watched all your drama auditions, and some of you were very promising. Others need some work."

She scans the room, and I move in my seat. I'm so not into acting. Rowena found me a monologue for my audition, and I memorized it and said it okay . . . but I'm sure I got in based on singing.

"First, let's go around the room and talk a little about ourselves." Miss Davis teeters by me. "Name, previous training and experience, and any other interesting tidbits you want to share."

Interesting tidbits? Check.

Miss Davis points to a girl who recites the names of thirty-seven interesting and worthwhile gifted performing arts programs she's attended since she was two. I try to think of something non-boring to say when it's my turn.

Hi, I'm Caitlin, and I was a homecoming princess last year.

I'm Cat, and I've gained and lost 300 pounds since I was twelve years old.

I have a restraining order against my ex, so let me know if you see him.

"I'm Gus," Armpit Guy says. "I went to Southwood performing arts magnet, and I was in three productions at Actor's Playhouse. I have two brothers, three sisters, a father, a mother, five sets of aunts and uncles, an *abuela* here and one back in Cuba, and a faithful dog, and not one of them can understand why I waste my time on this song-and-dance stuff instead of going into the family furniture business." He crosses his eyes. "Oh, and I'm the most talented guy in the room."

He's cute, and people laugh. A few guys yell stuff like, "Yeah, right" and "We'll see about that." The girl/guy ratio here is a little better than at the audition; maybe two to one instead of three to one. But still, if what Gigi says is true, it cuts the odds of romance considerably. *Good.*

The Piano-Playing Girl is next. "I'm Sylvanie. Not Sylvia, not Sylvania. Not Pennsylvania or Transylvania. Sylvanie." She then lists the usual five hundred community theater programs. I zone out again.

I can't act, but I can hit a high F. Here, I'll do it right now. Aaaaaahhhh!

When I come back to reality, Misty—a.k.a. Barnacle Girl—is enlightening us about how gifted she is.

"I was in the Miami Children's Theater summer program for the last two years. Last year, I had the lead in my school's production of *My Fair Lady*, so I decided to come here in hopes of finding some competition."

Her face says she thinks that's unlikely. Gigi mutters, "And I'm a bitch."

I giggle. I feel like Gigi and I have bonded.

Sean's next. He recites the same list of programs and mentions that he was in *My Fair Lady* too. He doesn't say which role, but he doesn't have to. Obviously the lead. "I'm a senior. I tried out as a freshman, but I had some family issues and couldn't go here. I'm really glad I could come this year. It's sort of a dream of mine."

"How cute," Gigi mutters, killing any solidarity I felt for her. Sean *is* cute—not that I'm thinking of him that way. I'm over guys. Besides, he's obviously taken by Barnacle Girl.

Gigi stands to introduce herself. "Gigi Correa."

Miss Davis looks at her roll book. "I don't have a Gigi here. Are you certain you got an acceptance from us?"

Gigi smiles. "Quite sure. Check if you have a Maria Georgina de la Iglesia Correa. But I prefer Gigi. Okay with everyone?" When Miss Davis nods, Gigi continues. "I'm from New York— the center of the universe. I understudied Young Eponine in the Broadway cast of *Les Miz*. I've done commercials for Band-Aids and Children's Tylenol. I went to La Guardia—the *real* High School of Performing Arts. Then divorce struck, and I moved to

Miami with the other refugees."

A few people react to *refugees*. The rest stare in awe. Then, since I'm sitting next to Gigi, they all turn to me. Wonderful.

"Um," I say. "I'm Caitlin. I like to sing. I've been in chorus since sixth grade. I sing opera. I like musical theater too, and . . . I'm really happy to be here."

That's it. I've told them nothing about myself and everything important. They don't know about Nick or about the whole humiliating homecoming princess debacle, or my mother. I could have said I'd sung at the Metropolitan Opera, and they'd have believed it. And it's amazing to be able to say I love opera and no one thinks it's weird. Okay, not *that* weird.

The rest of the period, we do improvisations. We play this game called Freeze and justify where two people start making up a scene. Then when they get into a funny position, someone yells, "Freeze!" They have to stop, and the person who called out takes one person's place in the scene and makes it a completely different situation. Most skits are funny, and a lot are . . . R-rated. Miss Davis doesn't seem to mind. I never yell, "Freeze!" Nothing I think of seems funny enough.

Finally, Miss Davis claps her hands. "Okay, that's it for today. Those who didn't participate this time will begin Wednesday. And there's homework."

Everyone groans, not just me.

"Art is suffering, children. Don't forget that. Wednesday, I want everyone to come prepared to act as their favorite animal."

Perfect.

Next is American History, a "regular" class—if a class can be regular when people start singing "I'm Only a Bill" from *Schoolhouse Rock* . . . and the teacher doesn't seem to mind. Gigi's in my Geometry class, and I practically fall over when she moves her books off the seat beside her for me to sit.

"You got lunch this period?" she asks after class. "We can sit together."

"Yeah." I skipped breakfast, and now my stomach feels tight.

When I get to my locker, Sean's just closing up his. "Hey, some morning," he says. "Want to sit with us at lunch?"

I take out my lunch bag. I'm about to ask him to sit with me and Gigi, when Misty bounces up. "Come on, Shawnee!" I'm invisible.

"Sorry," I say. "I told Gigi I'd sit with her."

"Some other time, then."

"Sure." I walk toward the cafeteria. Misty still hasn't noticed I'm there.

I was expecting the cafeteria to be like the scene in this old movie, *Fame*, which I rented twenty times, then pretended I'd lost so Mom would have to buy it from Blockbuster. It's about the New York City High School for the Performing Arts (the *real* one, as Gigi would say). In the movie, one guy starts playing the piano, then people start singing, dancing, drumming, until it was a huge production number about "Hot Lunch."

It's a little like that here, but not as organized. At one table, a group of art kids talk about "basic color principles" and use words like "chiaroscuro" with a brazen lack of fear of being beaten up. At another, some people look at sheet music and burst into song between bites of spaghetti.

I picture lunch at my old school. Peyton and Ashley are wearing their cheerleader outfits, just so people know who they're dealing with. If I was there, maybe I'd be wearing one too—my friends said they'd vote me on if I tried out. I wonder if there's a new girl sitting in my spot, wearing my uniform, maybe even flirting with my boyfriend (*ex*-boyfriend). If I could, would I go back?

"Caitlin, over here!"

Gigi's gesturing me toward her table. I think about what my friends would say about her. But then she wouldn't care. She wouldn't like them either. I sit.

"Having fun?" she says.

"Yeah. You're probably used to this from your old school."

A guy at the next table screams, "Fight for your manhood, you pathetic little vegetable!" I stare, startled, then realize they're reading a scene from a play.

I take out my yogurt. "My old school was way different." I look from the acting guy to the artists. I know the answer to my question. I don't want to go back to my old school. But I wonder if I could ever fit in with people here. They're so . . . free. Can I ever be like that?

"So, what'd you think of Drama?" Gigi asks.

I shrug. "It's my first class. Are we going to do any actual acting in there?"

"Actual acting?"

"Like, you know, from a script?"

"What? You're not *so* excited about coming in as your favorite animal?"

I shake my head, massively relieved she isn't going to give me some lecture about how this stuff *is* acting. "I just was sort of hoping to learn to play people first."

Gigi makes a scrunched-up face. "I'm not a pug, but I play one on TV." She squints at my lunch. "You're actually going to eat that?"

That's familiar, except my friends would like what I brought—nonfat yogurt and celery sticks. "What's wrong with it?"

"Nothing if you're an insect. But how are you going to get through Dance class on that? Here." She hands me an oatmeal cookie from her tray.

At the next table, someone starts some music, a sort of Latino fusion thing, really loud. A bunch of people start dancing a conga around the tables, and the guy named Gus actually gets *on* the table and reaches out to grab a girl to join them.

I take Gigi's cookie. She's right about Dance class. I'll be taking Dance three days a week here, instead of blowing off P.E., so I don't think a single cookie is going to turn me into the Thing That Ate the Universe.

I bite into it. I'm happier already.

After lunch is Dance. I'm happy that leotards are stretchy so that mine fits even after the *two* cookies I ended up eating (I went and bought another one).

"So where are you taking Dance?" Gigi asks while we're changing.

"What do you mean?"

"Like, where do you dance?" she repeats.

"Here," I say.

"No, but . . ." Gigi tugs on the strap of her silver leotard. "I mean, before this, where have you been taking? What's your studio?"

"Oh." I look away, so she can't see me starting to redden. Gigi's the kind of girl who *never* blushes and would look down on mere mortals who do. "I never took Dance before this. I mean, I took ballet-tap when I was five or something, and one time, my mom talked me into taking a hip-hop class because she thought I'd lose weight. Oh, and we play Dance, Dance Revolution in P.E., and . . ."

Shut up! Shut up!

"I don't take Dance," I finish.

"It's okay," Gigi says, sort of the way you'd talk to a four-year-old or an old lady or a cat, maybe. "You'll do fine."

• • • • •

Fine, I'm not. Actually, I suck. Our teacher, Ms. Wolfe (who weighs about ninety pounds—*hate* that!) has just demonstrated a totally impossible dance combination. I'm stumbling through it okay. But it's hard because there's this really irritating barking sound in my ear, like a deranged peke-a-poo. Something like *You! You!*

"You!"

Omigod! She means me. I stop dancing.

Me: Yes?

Ms. Wolfe: What is your name?

Me: Caitlin.

Ms. Wolfe: You need to pay attention, Caitlin. It's only the first day.

Misty (behind me): They really need to have a dance audition for this program.

My leotard, which fit fine over my butt in the dressing room, is crawling *inside* said butt, sent there by my formerly normal, currently sumo-sized tummy. Or maybe it's just trying to hide. I suck in my stomach.

Me: (Gulp)

Ms. Wolfe seems to be done with me anyway. The music starts up again, pulsing, pounding, and the whole routine repeats in fast-forward—stumblestumblestumble, youyouyou—except this time,

I am *very discretely* yanking my leotard from my butt.

The second time Ms. Wolfe stops us—um, me—she demonstrates the whole routine, making me follow. I'm the only one who didn't get this on the first try, so they're all watching—except Gigi, who is politely looking away.

"What a spaz!" Someone giggles behind me. "She dances like an opera singer."

Misty, again. I consider bumping her with my stomach, like a real sumo wrestler.

"Pay attention, Caitlin!" Ms. Wolfe says. "And don't forget your jazz hands."

"What are jazz hands?" *Was this something I was supposed to bring?*

As if on cue, every single hand in the class shoots up, fingers spread, just so I'll know I was the only one who didn't know this important bit of info.

"Oh," I say.

Several days later, the class ends.

"That was good," Gigi says. "You got it."

"I guess," I say. "But good luck remembering it Wednesday. You were incredible."

"Mom started me in Dance when I was doing pageants. That part was good at least. You really have to be a triple threat to make it in theater."

"What's a triple threat?"

"Someone who can do all three things—sing, dance, and act.

But I'm sure opera's different."

I see Sean leaving with Misty. I wave, but he doesn't seem to see me. I shrug. "Guess I'm only a single threat. Do you know where we could buy some cookies or something? I'm starved."

On the upside, I'm pretty sure cheerleading would also have been a bad idea.

On the other upside, I haven't sung yet. That's tomorrow. I'm looking forward to that.

♪ Opera_Grrrl's Online Journal

Subject: Dancing Fool
Date: August 17
Time: 4:34 p.m.
Feeling: Scholarly
Weight: 109 lbs. (Yeah, I gained 2 lbs. during the day—thx to 2 packs of GrandMa's oatmeal cookies I ate after dance class. Thx 2 Gigi for reminding me about cookies.)

3 great things about today☺

   1. Not having 2 take P.E.
   2. Getting a grade 4 singing
   3. Not having 2 see u-know-who in the halls

3 not-so-great things about today☹

1. Dance class
2. Dance class
3. Dance class

   I just remembered how *bad* I was at Dance, Dance Revolution in P.E. Who knew that was supposed 2 be *preparing* me for something?
   I don't miss my old school. OK, I can't make up funny armpit songs, and who ever heard of drama homework (I don't have a favorite animal. This 2 is Mom's fault. If she'd let me get the hamster I campaigned for in 3rd grade, I'd be fine now)? But for the 1st time in my life, I'm around people who like the same things I like.
   I just hope they don't all think I'm weird.

I hear Mom's car in the driveway. My mind races between two equal and opposite impulses: scream at her for letting me drop ballet-tap in first grade, setting me on a lifetime course of clumsiness and yo-yo dieting, or cry that she was right about the school. I don't belong there.

Both are equally appalling, so I stay put, keep the door shut, and think about . . . my favorite animal. Turtles are quiet and stay mostly in one place. They even hibernate.

I hear Mom puttering around the house. I know she wants me to come out and talk. Since that day I announced I'd move in with Dad if she didn't let me go to this school, we've had sort of an armed truce. She was mad as hell I'd used Dad to get what I wanted. But after she got over that, Mom was okay about the whole thing. She took me to buy leotards and got me a train pass. (She also insists on driving me to the train every single morning because she assumes I'll be raped and murdered—not necessarily in that order—if I take the bus. Guess I should be grateful, since it does give me an extra thirty minutes' sleep every morning.) Lately, she's almost seemed excited about my going to this school. Maybe she's actually interested in hearing about my first day. Maybe she *isn't* rooting for me to fail.

Yeah, and maybe I'll quit school and head straight for American Ballet Theatre.

I open the door and head for the kitchen.

"We're out of Healthy Choice," she announces tragically. She has that *Find a Husband After 35* book. It's open to a section called Packaging: Create Your Best Look.

My day was fine, thank you. And yours?

"Oh, well, I wasn't that hungry anyway. Should I make a salad?"

Mom wrinkles her nose. "No onions."

When I was a young fatgirl, we used to cook dinner together and talk. Mom was good at talking then. She was great at bad news. When I was picked last for P.E. or picked *on* during recess, we got along. It's good news she's terrible at.

"So, how was school?"

Again, I have this amazing urge to tell her. It was terrible. You were *soooo* right. But it wouldn't be worth the *I told you so's*. Besides, I'm not even sure how I feel yet.

"It was *funnnnn*," I say instead. "Everyone there's really color-ful and talented."

"That's great. Maybe you'll learn some things."

This bugs me. Then I wonder why. *Why?* I wanted to go to

learn things, right? "Yeah, I hope so. That's why I went."

"I know, hon. You're always so . . ." She takes a bite.

"So what?" I say.

"Nothing. Forget I said anything." She forks another bite.

"You didn't."

She pushes her plate away. "Caitlin, I don't have time to argue. Would you mind clearing the table? I have to finish getting dressed. I have a date."

I glance at her plate, then at the clock. Almost eight. Weird. Mom always makes sure guys buy her dinner. I don't say anything. It will be way better having her out of the house while I'm making whatever noises go with my favorite animal.

"Fine. No prob."

I finish my salad and start to clear the table. I eat the salad Mom left. After this act of piggery, my cell phone starts playing "March of the Toreadors." Caller ID reveals it's Peyton. I pick up the phone. I have to keep up with my friends in case performing arts school doesn't work out.

"Dude!" I easily slip back into my old persona. Who says I can't act?

"Is it terrible? Are you ready to come back to us where you belong?"

"It's great," I say, then realize she means living with Dad. "I mean, a lot better than I expected. Thing One and Thing Two have . . . um . . . junior peewee cheerleading four days a week, and with this new school, I hardly see them."

"Well, I'm glad you're having such a great time. We're destitute without you."

"*Desolate*, Peyton. You're desolate. Destitute means you're broke."

"Yah, like that's possible. Anyway, there's this new girl on the squad, and she thinks she's all that, sticking out her boobs and trying to be in charge." She keeps going, but I'm thumbing through Mom's *Find a Husband After 35* book.

Packaging: Create Your Best Look.

Advertising: Promote Your Personal Brand.

"So are there any cute guys there at least?" Peyton asks.

"Um, a few." I think of Sean Griffin's incredible eyes. "Well, at least one."

"That's good. I thought that guy at Wendy's might be the best player available. Such a loser. You're so sweet to be nice to people like that."

I laugh. "Oh, no, I didn't mean him."

"Saw Nick today."

"Yeah. So?"

"So nothing. He has a new car. A Beemer."

"Wow." I get a flash of memory. Nick behind the wheel of his old Mustang. I'm next to him, his arm around me. Not fat, not lonely. It was so easy being his girlfriend.

Except when it wasn't.

"So, is it a convertible?"

"Yeah, a roadster. They're like fifty thousand dollars, aren't they?"

I want to ask Peyton if there's some other girl, riding shotgun in that car. But instead, I tip Mom's salad plate into the sink and say, "So, what's your favorite animal?"

The second I get off the phone, the doorbell rings. Mom yells at me to get it.

I open the door to the toadiest-looking guy I've ever seen (and considering I live in Miami, where people go to die, that is saying a lot). This cannot possibly be Mom's date. He's wearing sandals with socks. I can see the outline of his undershirt through his shirt, and he's bald but he's combed hairs over the spot, as if no one will notice that way.

"You must be Katie," the Fashion Don't says.

"Caitlin, yes."

He sticks out his hand. "I'm Dr. Arnold Mikloshevsky."

Arnold? He's kidding, right? I mean, I know there's Arnold Schwarzenegger, but no mere mortal can get away with that name. Definitely not this guy.

Omigod! I sound like my mother. Maybe this guy has a beautiful soul.

Nah, Mom wouldn't date someone with a beautiful soul. He must have money.

I take his hand. It's damp. "Nice to meet you, Doctor."

"Arnold."

"Arnold." *Ah-nohd.* "Mom will be out any second." But I'm thinking life as we know it has ceased. My mother, shallowest puddle in the rainstorm, is actually dating someone . . . clammy.

He looks me up and down. Well, down anyway. His eyes stop at my chest, and I realize I'm still wearing my leotard. "So you're a dancer?"

Still looking. *Come on, guy. You're short, but you're not that short.*

"Um, not exactly." I cross my arms over my chest. "Mom!"

"I'll be right there!" she sings.

A sudden, horrific thought occurs to me. Oh. My. God. She didn't want onions because she's planning to kiss this guy.

"So, what kind of doctor are you?"

"Podiatrist."

"Podiatrist. That's . . . ?" *Rear ends?*

"The foot. Conditions of the foot. Calluses, fungi, bone spurs." He looks down. "But a young thing like you wouldn't have to worry about any of that."

"I'll see what's taking Mom."

But that's when she shows up.

It sounds clichéd to say that my jaw drops when she walks in. But my jaw does, literally, drop. She has on a pink-and-white-checked fake Chanel suit with a skirt which, while short, would cover her underwear—even if she bent over. She has her hair and makeup all done like a flight attendant at the Dallas airport, instead of like an exotic dancer. In fact, her whole ensemble is classic, conservative, and . . . well, classy. Her nails are French-manicured and not one bit of her glitters.

Packaging, indeed . . .

She holds out her hand to Dr. Toe-Jam. "Shall we?"

"Valerie, I had no idea . . ."

"Yes?" She looks at him, like, *Adore me*!

"When you mentioned your daughter, I pictured a little girl, not such a lovely young woman."

Annoyance flickers across her face, just like anytime someone compliments me. But this particular time, I'm right with her. I'm as grossed out as she is, but for different reasons. Is she actually going to let him touch her?

"You must have been a child bride," he continues.

That helps. "Oh, well, that's true. I was married when I was only twenty."

"Which explains why you two look like sisters."

"Hmmm, which of us is the prettier sister?"

I make my escape. "It was great meeting you, Dr. Mikloshevsky." I look at Mom like, *Are you sure about this?* "I have a ton of homework."

And then I go to my room and sing until my lungs hurt.

♪ Opera_Grrrl's Online Journal

Subject: Chasing My Tail
Date: August 20
Time: 5:10 p.m.
Listening 2: "Vesti la giubba" (sad clown aria from Pagliacci)
Feeling: Seriously bummed
Weight: 110 lbs. (Cookies! Cookies!)

1st week's almost over. Picture the next 3 days being pretty much like the 1st. People here aren't like @ Key Biscayne, but the laws of the jungle still apply. Every1 hangs w/their own kind. At Key, that meant lions w/lions and gazelles w/gazelles. Here, it's more like hyenas w/hyenas and warthogs w/warthogs. Every1's funny and different and special . . . . except me. I'm standard issue . . . . like a yellow Lab. Or a mutt.

    Speaking of dogs . . . . I spent hours prepping for My Favorite Animal, based on this little dog our neighbors used 2 have. Silky. I *was* that dog, prancing around in my jeweled collar, chasing my own tail. Then I got 2 class.

    1st off, hardly any1 chose anything as boring as a dog. Gigi (I HATE HER!) was a sea anemone, and Gus scored BIG by doing a baby kangaroo, fighting its way up 2 its mother's nipple. The only other person who did a dog—Misty—was *waaay* more creative than me. She pretended her dog had on 1 of those cone collars they put on pets 2 keep them from chewing their stitches or whatever. Then she played a dog w/a compulsion 2 scratch . . . . and got a standing O.

    So, of course, I had 2 follow her.

    I was chasing my tail, all right. I think I even saw Miss Davis yawn☹.

*F*riday afternoon, instead of Dance (a.k.a. the third circle of hell), we get called into the auditorium. "I hear they do this all the time," Gus says on the way in. "Pull us out of class to watch some program that's supposed to be good for us. Gives us a chance to catch up on all that sleep we're missing, having to catch the bus here at six-thirty."

I shrug. "To get out of Dance, I'd watch eye surgery."

Gus grins. "Hey, you wouldn't be bad at it if you'd just loosen up." He grabs my arm and pulls me toward him like Antonio Banderas with Madonna in *Evita*. He tries to dip me, sending me crashing to the floor. Crowds run for cover, and I think one girl screams. But maybe that was me.

"Take your seats everyone!" It's Rowena onstage, and I try to scramble up before she sees it's me. But that just means I almost knock someone down. Specifically Misty.

"Watch it!" she says. "Do you get off on hurting people?"

I ignore her. "See?" I tell Gus. "I'm hopeless."

I wait for him to agree with me, but he says, "Nah, you're not hopeless. You just got to shake it, baby. You should dance with us at lunch."

"Take your seats quickly." Rowena sees me. "Caitlin, are you okay?"

"Yeah, sorry." I half-stand and slink to the seat Gigi's holding. "I am so glad you'll still be seen with me after that."

Gigi laughs. "No Dance today. Be happy."

I am. For about three seconds. Then I think about what Gus said about dancing with them at lunch. Does everyone think I'm a snob because I don't do stuff like that? Don't they realize there are people on the planet who don't want to be the center of attention at all times?

I glance over at Gus, who's grabbed another willing girl and is doing the cha-cha, yelling "one, two, cha-cha-cha!" *Guess not.*

Finally, when everyone has settled down, Rowena says, "I thought it might be interesting for you to watch. The college-level students are having auditions for *La Traviata.*"

Groans. Gnashing of teeth. Opera's no normal teenager's favorite thing, not even here. I, being abnormal, am instantly excited. I've heard that the college Opera Workshop program, which is held on the same campus as the high school, is really great.

"Any duels in it?" a guy asks.

"Can we go to Dance?" this girl, Kimberley, who's an incredible dancer, asks.

"No, we'll be here today."

"Cool idea," Sean says. "After all, we'll be in college soon too."

I hear someone mutter, "Suck up," behind me. I agree. Sean hasn't said a single word to me since Monday. He just hangs out with his old friends all the time and acts like he's better than everyone else. I don't get it. He was so friendly at my audition.

Rowena's having all the tenors and sopranos audition by singing the *"Brindisi,"* a drinking song from the first act, where the two main characters flirt with each other.

La Traviata is my all-time favorite opera. I discovered it years ago, when Mom was watching this movie *Pretty Woman*. Julia Roberts plays a hooker who gets hired by a millionaire played by Richard Gere. In one scene, Richard takes Julia to the opera to see *La Traviata*, which is about a woman of ill repute, Violetta, who falls for this guy, Alfredo, then leaves him when his family disapproves—then dies of tuberculosis. (They used the same plot in *Moulin Rouge,* with Nicole Kidman.) Julia loves it (and Richard), and in the big final scene, Richard drives down her street in his convertible, playing *"Dammi tu forza, o cielo"* on the car stereo, climbs Julia's fire escape, and they live happily ever after.

I loved that scene. I cried. I begged Mom to buy the movie so I could hear the music over and over. She bought it because she wanted to do her hair like Julia Roberts. It wasn't until three years later when I started taking voice, and Rowena took a bunch of us to a dress rehearsal for *La Traviata* at the Florida Grand Opera, that I knew where it was from. I bought the CD and listened to it a million times.

Anyway . . . back in the real world.

The girl onstage is the third to sing. She's a fatgirl, about forty pounds overweight, but beautiful, and has a lot of control in the difficult middle range of her voice and what's more, she *seems* like Violetta—really strong and in charge of her destiny, which, of course, is what makes the story so tragic. If Violetta had lived today, she wouldn't be a hooker. She'd be the CEO of IBM.

"She *looks* like an opera singer," the blond surfer dude behind me whispers. "All she needs are the horns."

A girl agrees. "Right. *Moooooo.*"

I give them a look, but I know they're right. The girl onstage is the best Violetta so far, but she wouldn't be real convincing as someone dying of a wasting disease. My jeans feel tight, and I think of the pizza Gigi talked me into at lunch. Some girls I know would go and stick a finger down their throats, but that is one particular disorder I've managed to avoid. I'll do better this weekend. Should be easy, as I no longer have a social life. I'm sure my friends have forgotten me completely.

The pair onstage finish, and Rowena says, "That it for sopranos and tenors?"

No one volunteers. Seán raises his hand. "Can we try? I mean, just for fun."

Rowena checks her watch. "Can I get a soprano to go with you?"

Gigi nudges me. "You should go."

"What? No! Why?"

"Because you're really good. You've seen what everyone else can do—show them what you can do."

If someone at my old school had said that, I'd figure they were trying to make me look bad. But even though I've only known Gigi a few days, I think she means it.

Sean's making his way to the stage, and next thing I know, my hand's up in the air.

And so are Rowena's eyebrows. She knows I get scared. "Looks like we do have a volunteer." I see that Misty also has her hand up, but Rowena's pointing to me. I stand and walk to the front of the room.

But now that I've raised my hand and committed, I worry I'll look like a show-off. *Why did I volunteer?* To impress Sean, the unimpressible? No. It's just what Gigi said—to show the rest of them I'm actually good at something, even if it's not what they think's a big deal. After screwing up in Drama and Dance all week, I need to do that.

But I can't think about that now, because the accompanist starts playing, and Sean begins to sing, and suddenly, I'm no longer here. I'm at a beautiful party in Paris. I forget all the people in the auditorium, the bored faces, the dance class I'll have to go back to on Monday, even Sean's cologne . . . soap . . . whatever. Now, I *am* Violetta.

Sean starts his last lines. His voice is as good on the opera stuff as it was on musical theater:

Let us drink, for with wine,
Love will enjoy yet more passionate kisses.

I take a deep breath and sing:

In life, everything is folly
Which does not bring pleasure

I visualize myself as sparkling, popular, beautiful, and beloved. Sean is Alfredo, totally hot for me. I smile at him and remember everything Rowena taught me. I focus my voice in the mask of my face (what zit cream commercials call the T-zone) and remember to breathe, and my voice just flows out of me. I know I sound great. I sound perfect. But will people here get it, or will they think it's lame? Sean and I finish the song together, and the college students who were auditioning explode with applause. They get it, at least. I stand a few seconds, enjoying it, living it.

When I get back to my seat, Gigi grins and holds up her hand to high-five me. A minute later, the guy behind me, the surfer dude who made the comment about the horns, leans over and says, "Wow. If opera singers look like you, I'll go to the opera."

I don't answer. Gigi says, "That was supposed to be a compliment, Cait."

I smile. "Thanks."

"You're welcome. I'm Rex, by the way. Remember me when you're a star."

Rowena's saying something about upcoming talent, which makes me blush and squirm some more. Then she starts calling up baritones. Sean's sitting on the other side of the auditorium. I figure maybe he'll say something to me on the way out. But when we go, he walks out the opposite side door. The girl who sang before me stops me, though. "You were incredible. You'll be some competition for us soon."

I can't stop grinning. "Thanks. You were great too."

"Hey, us opera girls gotta stick together."

I smile some more. She smiles. I smile all the way to music theory class.

At least I'm best at one thing, the thing I love best.

♪ Opera_Grrrl's Online Journal

Subject: I got 2 sing at school!!!
Date: August 21
Time: 5:35 p.m.
Listening 2: "Brindisi" from La Traviata
Feeling: Happy
Weight: 109 lbs. (I've decided 2 leave my wallet @ home so I can't buy food at school)

The thing I love about singing opera is: when you're doing it, it's all you can think of . . . . so you're not thinking about how:

1. You still have 2 go 2 dance class 3x a week.
2. You might gain back 40 lbs. any day now.
3. It's Friday and you have no friends 2 do anything with.
4. Your mother's dating a podiatrist!

Mom's new bf, Arnold, took her out 2x this week + breakfast yesterday a.m. When I got home today, she was pacing the living rm in hot rollers . . . . . . cell phone at her hip, and her portable in her hand, like a dr. waiting for word on an emergency surgery. "I'm expecting a phone call," she said in case I had any doubt.

I have no plans for 2nite except 2 stay home and pretend I'm Violetta, set 4 my date with Alfredo . . . . I'm sort of ok with that.

Unbelievable! Mom just knocked on the door. I figured she was just complaining about the noise, but she asked me if I wanted 2 go out 2 dinner. She called Arnold and he said he had 2 work late so no date.

I was nice. I didn't point out that she always says *never* 2 call guys . . . . . . Mom has tons of "rules" for dating, rules she got from books. Don't ask guys out. Don't accept a date with a guy on 2-short notice. And one of her big, big rules is NEVER call guys. In Mom-world, a girl who calls a guy might as well show up in English class and give him a lap dance.

I also didn't point out that working late sounded like a lame excuse. (Aren't I nice?) Obviously, if she was suggesting dinner w/her fat daughter, she must be . . . . fragile.

> So I suggested Hard Rock b/c it's the loudest place I know & we won't have 2 talk. She agreed, so maybe she had the same idea.

I'm on my way to the door when my cell rings.

It's Peyton. "Hey, Cait, what are you doing tonight?"

"Nothing much. What are you doing?"

"Oh, you know . . . first game of the year, so we're cheering. You could be too if you'd stuck around."

"I know. Don't remind me." I try to sound appropriately regretful.

"Maybe you can come to the game," she says.

I sigh. If there's one good thing about this new school, it's that I get to miss seeing You Know Who at football games. "I wish I could, but I'm meeting some friends for dinner at Hard Rock. Can I call you tomorrow?"

Dead silence on the other end.

Sometimes it's just easier to lie.

So I just had to get out of the house this morning. Mom's moping around—no call from Arnold today—and when the clock hit eight, she called Dad to scream about yet another late child-support check. So hoping to kill, but not *literally* kill, the two hours before my voice lesson, I went to this French bakery on Crandon Boulevard to drink coffee and write an essay for English class.

Key Biscayne is a Starbucks-Free Zone. But I guess everyone must've gone off-island to get their caramel macchiato fix today, because there's only one person at the bakery when I walk in—the one person I'm avoiding more than anyone.

After we broke up, I'd look for Nick's car before I went anyplace, to avoid him. But he got a new car, and I never asked what color it is, so now I can't.

He's sitting, writing in a notebook. He doesn't see me. Yet. You'd think I'd enjoy rejecting Nick, after what he did to me; enjoy it like you enjoy slapping a mosquito and seeing it, smashed, still full of your own blood. But it's not like that. I don't want to crush Nick. I just want to forget him. I want to turn around, to leave, to *run* even, but as soon as I start to go, I hear his voice.

"You don't have to leave, you know."

I turn back. "What?"

"I won't bother you. I have class at nine, so I'm going soon. And I meant what I said last time—I'm leaving you alone. So if you want to sit and . . . drink your tea, you can." He looks down at his book and shrugs. "Or not. Whatever." He goes back to reading, ignoring me.

After that, it seems silly to leave. I go to the counter and order my tea (How did he remember about the tea?) because I have a voice lesson later. I decide to get a black-and-white cookie too, because I ran out of the house too quick to get breakfast—which you're supposed to eat or you get fatter, right? I stand there, trying not to look at him.

But when you try not to look at someone, it's impossible to look at anything else. My eyes keep going to Nick, the way they used to in seventh-grade Science class, when I sat two rows behind him. I couldn't take my eyes off him then either.

Don't stare. He's still writing in the notebook. I remember Nick used to write—not just homework either. He wrote me poems—amazing poems. Right now he has a book beside him. He doesn't look up, doesn't meet my eyes, but I'm sure he sees me seeing him. Even after all this time, I can't get over his looks. Just like in seventh grade, only hotter. He has these green eyes that stand out against his dark skin and hair, and they seem like they could look right through you. I never quite believed anyone as hot as Nick would be into someone like me. I think that's partly why I made so many excuses for him—for the way he treated me, even when he hit me the first time. Well, that and the poetry. It was incredible, finding out someone in the "it" crowd had a poetic soul.

I'm fumbling for my pen, but I'm looking at the way the bottom of his hair meets the top of his cheekbone. He's wearing a white T-shirt that is shocking beside his brown skin. I know how it would smell if I got closer, like bleach and Calvin Klein cologne, with just a hint of the beach where he lives.

And if I close my eyes, I can feel his fist, smashing into my face.

Keep that thought. That's a good thought.

"Hey! Your tea."

I see Nick's eyes flicker up. I turn away, feeling my whole body start to sweat.

"Thanks." I take my tea. "Um, do you have a pen I can borrow?"

"I only have one, and that's for the register. I could look in back." It's obvious he doesn't want to.

"No, no, that's okay. I'll just read."

I take my stuff and sit. I rifle through my purse again because, of course, I can't write an essay without a—

"Need a pen?"

Of course, it's Nick.

"It's okay." I feel like taking something from him will get me all involved.

"I have an extra one. It's just a Bic from the drugstore. It doesn't . . . obligate you in any way."

"That's not it," I snap.

"Then take it." He's holding it out, a plain old Bic Round Stic pen. "I don't need it back. I'm leaving in five minutes, okay?"

"I can give it back." I realize, after saying this, I'm saying I'll take it.

"No biggie. It's a cheap pen. Besides, I know you'll bite it and get it all disgusting." He says it like he's grossed-out but he's smiling. "You still do that?"

"I try not to." I walk over, holding out my hand for the pen. I catch the title of his book, *The Batterer: A Psychological Profile*. He sees me looking at it and, quick as he can, takes his hand and slides the book under the table.

I don't meet his eyes, but I'm still thinking about that title, *The Batterer*. I know that battery is technically what Nick did to me. But I never thought he knew it, that he admitted it to himself. Part of me wants to turn away now.

But my hand closes around the pen. "Thanks," I say.

"No problem." He sees that I'm still looking at his lap, the book. "I'm . . . uh, I'm in that class, the one you put me in."

He means the Family Violence class the judge put him in after I got the restraining order against him. I say, "I thought it was only for six months," then regret saying anything. He probably screwed up and had to repeat it.

"I didn't screw up," he says, again reading my thoughts. "I signed up to retake the class voluntarily. I started . . . it took me until the end to . . . really realize why I was there and . . . what I did to you." Now, *he's* trying not to look at *me*, like he's afraid of me instead of the other way around. "Anyway, I'm repeating it, so I can actually learn to be different. My counselor, Mario, says you can't let anger run your life. You know?"

He looks at me now. I still haven't said anything. Part of me still wants to get away from him. The other part, a big, big part, wants to touch him, wants to tell him it's okay. But I remember what my own counselor said about guys' lies. So I just nod.

He shrugs. "Anyway, I'm going to class in *one* minute. And I said I wouldn't bother you, so I guess I should just shut the hell up now." He starts picking his things up, closing the notebook and putting it into his lap before picking the book up again. He sticks his pen into the spiral of the notebook. He nods, then stands up.

You must speak. Failing to speak gives him way too much importance.

"Um, thanks for the pen."

"No problem. By the way . . ." He points out the window at a white convertible. "That's my car, if you need to avoid me in the future."

"It's . . . nice."

"My dad would hardly have something lame out in the drive-way, right?"

He doesn't wait for an answer. He's out the door. I watch him getting in the car, and I feel the motion in my legs, like I'm running toward him. I don't. I take out my notebook and start writing—not the essay for English class, but an entry for my journal. I'm writing in my notebook, but I'll transfer it when I get home.

♪ Opera_Grrrl's Online Journal

Subject: Why does she stay w/ him???
Date: August 22
Time: 8:35 a.m.
Feeling: Nervous
Weight: 109 lbs.

When people hear about a girl getting beat up by her bf, they always say the same thing: Why does she stay w/ him? What is she, stupid or something? Does she like it? If some guy hit me, I'd just leave. It should be that easy.

News flash: It isn't. When it happens 2 you, it's like you're so far in2 it before you even realize what's going on.

1st off, guys don't hit girls on the first date. I was in counseling w/ 10 other girls, and not one of them got hit before they were really, really . . . . involved. I mean, there are signs, warning signs . . . "Controlling behaviors," Lucia, my shrink, called them. Like, when he tells you not 2 hang w/ your friends

---

anymore (that's how I traded my lifelong friends for Peyton and Ashley), and makes you call him the second you get home, like 2 prove you're actually *there* & not someplace else. But Nick— and other guys, I'm sure—always made that kind of thing sound so *reasonable* like he was just concerned for my welfare. So you excuse it. Any1 would.

And 2nd, even when he *does* hit you, he's all apologetic. He's saying he'll *die* if you break up w/him, and you believe him b/c by that time, you know how crummy his life is. You know his mom ditched him when he was 5, and his father has never said 1 nice thing 2 him his whole life. So it's no wonder he doesn't trust people. Who would??? And you always feel like if you could just do a better job at letting him know how much you love him, he wouldn't be that way. So you say you'll TRY and he does 2.

And 3rd, more than feeling sorry for him, you . . . LOVE him. I loved Nick. Maybe I still do. I know it's pathetic . . . . I thought he loved me, but maybe he didn't even know who I really was.

There's 4th & 5th & 6th 2, but those come later. The first 3 are why girls—lots of girls, not just me—don't "just leave" the second it happens. It's why we're stupid. And that's why it's so easy 2 look into those big green eyes of his and forget how he *always* said he'd change, forget everything except how good it was when it was good. But I can't forget the other stuff. I have 2 make myself remember.

*A*ttack the high notes from above," Rowena says after my tenth unsuccessful run-through of the Mozart piece I'm practicing.

"What do you mean, from above?"

Rowena moves Fred the cat over so she can reach the sheet music, then points to a high B. "See that?" When I nod, she says, "Now close your eyes and visualize it."

"Right." I close my eyes. Rowena has a weird way of looking at things. "I'm visualizing."

"Picture your voice as a physical being, floating above those notes. So instead of having to reach to get them, you're dive-bombing from above."

"Okay."

"What does your voice look like?"

"Um, a pink line?" I wasn't really visualizing, but now I am.

"Excellent."

She starts to play my piece, and I start singing. But this time,

I picture my voice dancing above the staff. It works. The music's easier and it sounds better.

"Excellent job," Rowena says when I'm finished.

"I wish everything was that easy—just visualize it, and it happens." I'm thinking about Nick; how seeing him made me sort of want things back like they were before, thinking about how lonely I feel.

"Maybe it is."

I visualize Nick exploding into a bazillion ex-boyfriend pieces. Better yet: I visualize Misty exploding. I grin.

Rowena looks at the clock. My hour's over. "So, how do you like the school?"

"It's great. But the kids there think I'm weird."

"Really? Are you sure you're not projecting, that you're not the one who thinks they're weird?"

I visualize Gus and his conga line, the part of me that wants to join in with them, and the part that doesn't. Do I not want to dance because I think I'll look stupid? Or because I think they look stupid?

I visualize myself, conga-ing. *No way.*

"I was surprised when you sang yesterday in the auditorium," Rowena says. "It was really brave of you. Sometimes, you have to be brave to be an artist."

I think of Nick again.

"I'm brave a lot," I say.

Subject: All That Jazz
Date: August 24
Time: 5:22 p.m.
Listening 2: "All That Jazz" from Chicago
Feeling: Happy
Weight: 114 lbs. (That is *so* not possible. I weighed 109 Fri., and I'm STARVING.)

After school, some of us walked over 2 the train station 2gether. I was walking w/ Gigi, making fun of how the dancers all walk in 3rd position ALL THE TIME so they look like penguins . . . . . and someone started singing "All That Jazz" from Chicago, just singing, right on the street like Peyton and Ashley said. No one acted like she was weird. They joined in. It was the middle of the day downtown, and these guys in suits with stressed-out faces were looking at us like we were on drugs. But by the time we got 2 "No, I'm no one's wife, but oh, I love my life!" I was singing 2. It was like being in a musical, and I was one of those people!

It was the first time I felt like, maybe, I could belong at this school.

*P*icture the next three weeks, being a replay of the first one. Fast-forward through visuals of me, dancing badly, me, playing the piano badly, me, acting like various furry or feathered creatures or inanimate objects, me, hardly singing at all, and me, hanging with Gigi, who is almost always eating and whose hair has now taken on a pinkish hue. Picture my weight going up and down on a daily basis. Picture Sean, not saying hi to me because, I guess, I don't rate. Also picture me, not having much to do on the weekends, and sitting home Saturday nights watching *Cops* with Mom.

Picture lots of oatmeal cookies (I've discovered this place called The Pit, where they have machines that sell them).

Picture Dr. Toe-Jam, ignoring Mom a lot of the time. Picture her acting all depressed. Then picture them at our house Tuesday night, Wednesday night, acting like newlyweds.

"It's weird," I tell Gigi the Wednesday after the third Tuesday this happens. "He doesn't take her out on weekends, and she gets so mad I assume they're breaking up. Then he shows up on a Tuesday."

We're on the train. Since I live only one stop from Gigi, we've been meeting up each morning. She gets off at my station, waits for me on the platform, and we get back on together.

Gigi takes a bite of her salt bagel. "He's probably married."

"Married?"

"Duh. This is a surprise, Cait? You were thinking, what . . . he's a secret agent?"

I giggle, picturing Arnold as James Bond. "No, he's definitely not hot enough." I stop laughing and think. "I don't know. It's weird."

"My mom dated a married guy when we first moved here. He was the same way. He'd take her out during the week—probably told his wife he was working late. Then on weekends, we never heard from him. He'd say he was out of town or something."

"Wow. How'd she find out?"

Gigi takes another bite of her bagel and talks with her mouth full. "We saw him at Bloomies with his wife. Man, was that ugly!" A couple of women sitting near us glare at her. I don't know if it's because of the see-food or because she's talking so loud, but Gigi glares back. "We were shopping for sheets, and there he was. Mom goes up to him, and he pretends he doesn't know who she is, like he thought she was a saleswoman or something. He actually asked which towels were more absorbent. Mom's trying to figure out why, when this big blond woman shows up. She says, 'Jeff, do you prefer the peach towels or the apricot?'"

Gigi says it in this snooty accent, like a cartoon rich lady, and I try not to laugh.

She continues. "So I say I like the peach best, and can we paint my room that color when Mom and I move in. That's when he starts looking for security. His wife's going, 'Jeff? Jeff? What did she mean by that?' and I go, 'But you told me we would be a real family as soon as you got rid of your old bat of a wife.'"

That's when I lose it. "I'm sorry," I say. "I was just picturing it. I know it's not funny."

"It's totally funny. It was like one of those improvs we do in Davis's class. And then the Bloomies security guy shows up, and Jeff tells him to get us away from him. The guy looks at Jeff like he's nuts. 'I'm supposed to guard the *towels*, Mister.'"

Now Gigi's cracking up too. "The next day, Jeff calls and tries to explain—like that's possible. I'm proud to say Mom told him to piss off."

"Good for her."

"Yeah." Gigi gets serious. "But she was real sad. She felt stupid that she got used that way, like she should've known better. Anyway, that's when I let her talk me back into pageants for a while. I figured it would get her talking about something besides what jerks she thinks men are."

The train rumbles toward our stop, and the guy announces it on the P.A. system.

"I can't believe my mom would go for a married guy," I yell above the noise.

"Tell me about it. I couldn't either. Maybe all men *are* jerks."

Just as she says that, the announcement ends, so she's scream-ing, *"All men are jerks!"* into the quiet car. Everyone stares.

For their benefit, I say, "No comment," and we both crack up.

But I'm thinking that sounds about right. All my life, Mom's been trying to impress some guy—first my dad, then other guys. She even flirts with guys *I* bring home. It's like love is a competi-tive sport for her and she needs to win to feel good.

But all my life, she's never dated anyone like Arnold.

"Next Monday," Miss Davis announces after an intense hour of pretending we're trees, "we will hold auditions for our first per-formance of the year. It will be a revue with a theme of Welcome to New York."

Sylvanie already has her hand up. "Will new people have a chance, or will you all just be rewarding the seniors for the time they've put in?"

"We've chosen the revue format to showcase as many students as possible. Those not chosen to perform individually will partici-pate in the group numbers."

Group numbers. Which presumably means—*gulp!*—dancing.

I raise my hand. "Do we have to do the group numbers if we don't get a solo?"

Miss Davis nods. "Everyone will want to participate in the group numbers to gain experience. Remember, there are no small parts—only small actors."

Okay. I look like a diva who doesn't want a small part. There's no way for me to turn back the too-swift hands of time and explain what I meant. I'm stuck with it.

Oh, well. No solo for me. Hopefully, they'll let me dance in back.

I'm in the bathroom between classes, when I hear a voice through the stall door.

"What are you planning for auditions?"

It sounds like Misty. But since Misty's never actually spoken to me, except to rag on my dancing, it's hard to be sure. Two girls are practicing a scene from *The Crucible* in the other two stalls (I've gotten used to the fact that people do plays at all times here, so when the first girl screamed, "Yellow bird!" I didn't flinch). She must be talking to them. I go back to what I was doing.

"Hey, Caitlin, you in there?" Misty bangs on the door of my stall.

I flush and come out. "Don't know. Something classical. Or maybe what I did for my audition—this song from *Phantom*."

Misty sits on the bathroom counter, and spits on her eye makeup brush to get it wet. Mom would be *soooo* appalled. I've heard Misty sing by now, and she has one of those breathy soprano voices chorus teachers love because they blend (I don't blend) but she's not hugely talented. Just okay.

"How about you?" I say.

Misty's wrinkling her nose so bad I think it's an allergic reaction to the makeup. "I don't know, Cait. Do you really think you should?"

Cait? "Why not?"

She shrugs. "Well, you probably know best."

"No. Tell me what you mean."

"Oh, I don't know. I was in this program where they took a bunch of us to Broadway shows." She takes out a blue eyeliner pencil and turns her eyelid inside out to draw a line under her eye. "And all the revues were pretty jazzy. I just don't know if that long-hair opera stuff will fly. You know?"

"I don't know." I totally do know, actually. I was wondering about it myself.

"I mean," Misty continues, "*we* understand music like that. But do the vulgar masses? Maybe people here would be more interested in hanging with you if you didn't always do stuff like that, act like you're better than them."

She's right. I rocked in class the other day, but I still feel like I'm a different species. Before I can think of an answer, she finishes her other eye, looks at her watch, and says, "Oh, gotta go to class."

She hurries off, and I head in the opposite direction.

I hear Mom's key in the lock, and for the first time in— ohhhhh, my whole life maybe, I run to see her. I want to tell her Gigi's theory, so she can dump this loser. "Hey, Mom."

She's dressed like her old self today—must have been a non-Arnold lunch. Denim micro-mini, pink platform sandals, and two toe-rings.

"Hi, Caitlin. I'm in sort of a hurry." She looks toward her bedroom.

"Date with Arnold?"

"Yes, I need to get ready. He'll be here any—"

"That's what I want to talk to you about. Arnold takes you out on weekdays, but never Fridays. He calls at weird times. He never buys you dinner." I'm talking faster now, picturing Gigi and her mom in the towel department. "Do you think maybe—"

"He's married, Caitlin." She's looking at her watch. "That's why we can't go out weekends. He has to be with his wife."

"But . . . you *know* he's married."

"Of course. I'm not stupid. I know the warning signs. I read Dear Abby."

My mouth is so wide open I can feel air hitting my tonsils, my uvula, my lymph glands. "But . . . so how come you're still dating him?"

"Every man since your father was afraid of commitment. They had to concentrate on their careers or take care of a sick mother, or they were just too much man for any one woman. Arnold doesn't have those hang-ups. He's already made a commitment."

"Yeah. To someone else."

"Not really. If he was committed to her, he wouldn't be seeing me."

"But . . ." Her reasoning is a tennis ball being whacked back and forth.

"I'm not getting any younger, Caitlin. I want a husband before I'm old and fat. It hasn't worked with single men. Maybe this will be better."

"But . . ." I still don't feel capable of more than the one word.

"Don't you want the same things everyone else around here has? Your father sure isn't providing them." She looks at the door again. "Besides, he's really a sweet man."

Okay. Now I have words. "He's a scumbag who's cheating on his wife."

She shakes her head. "You don't know what it's like. Sometimes you can be really lonely, even when you're married to someone." She picks up her purse, a black one with little dogs all over it. "Look, I need to get ready. He's coming soon." She starts toward her bedroom.

"But Mom . . ." I'm about to say she obviously hasn't read the same Dear Abby columns I've read, the ones that say married guys will just go back to their wives. Or the ones that say mothers should set a good example for their daughters, for that matter.

"Yes?"

I shake my head. "Nothing." I can't say that stuff to her. It would be like calling her a slut. But I can't believe that. I'd rather believe she's just stupid, like Brianna Owens in the luggage rack of the bus. Maybe sluts are really just stupid girls who want love. "Just wondered if you went shopping."

"There's some Healthy Choice in the fridge." She starts to leave the room.

I say, "Can I take the car? I want to buy some salad stuff."

"Sure." She fumbles in her purse, then tosses me the keys. "That's a good idea. It looks like you've put on some weight since you started this new school."

I take the keys and drive myself to KFC. I can't believe she's dating someone who is married. *On purpose.* It's just so . . . wrong. On the way there, I see Nick's car at the French bakery again. I think about going in. *Would it really be so bad?* He's in counseling. But I remember what my therapist said. She said once a vase is broken, you can't fix it, not really, and that's what it's like with relationships too. So I ride on.

Subject: Bart Simpson
Date: September 16
Time: 6:15 p.m.
Listening 2: Cast recording of Hairspray
Feeling: Confused
Weight: 117 lbs.

I've given myself one of those assignments Bart Simpson gets at school, where his teacher makes him write something 50 times so he won't do it again. Here goes:

I will not think of Nick. I will not think of Nick. I will not think of Nick. I will not think of Nick. I will not think of Nick. I will not think of Nick. I will not think of Nick. I will not think of Nick. I will not think of Nick. I will not think of Nick. I will not think of Nick. I will not think of Nick.

Iwillnotthinkofnickiwillnotthinkofnickiwillnotthinkofnick iwillnotthinkofnickwillnotthinkofnickiwillnotthinkofnickiwill notthinkofnickwillnotthinkofnickiwillnotthinkofnickiwillnot thinkofnickwillnotthinkofnickiwillnotthinkofnickiwillnot thinkofnickwillnotthinkofnickiwillnotthinkofnickiwillnot thinkofnickwillnotthinkofnickiwillnotthinkofnickiwillnot thinkofnickwillnotthinkofnickiwillnotthinkofnickiwillnot thinkofnickwillnotthinkofnickiwillnotthinkofnickiwillnot thinkofnickwillnotthinkofnickiwillnotthinkofnickiwillnot thinkofnickwillnotthinkofnickiwillnotthinkofnickiwillnot thinkofnickwillnotthinkofnickiwillnotthinkofnick.

Doesn't work for Bart either.

So what are you thinking of doing for auditions?" Rowena asks at my voice lesson Saturday. "*Phantom?*"

"I'm tired of that."

Rowena raises an eyebrow, but doesn't say anything. "How about this then?" She points to the Mozart piece I've been practicing.

I shake my head. "I was thinking of this." I take out the vocal selections from *Hairspray,* a rock opera on Broadway based on an old cult movie.

Rowena looks doubtful. "I have to say, this doesn't completely sound like you." Fred the cat jumps onto the keyboard and glares at my music.

"The girl in this song has a weight problem," I say. "Besides, I want to change my image." I pet Fred's head.

"Interesting. You know, I was talking to Ms. Wolfe about you the other day."

"Let me guess—she thinks I should change my major to dance."

I don't even get a smile from her. "Actually, she was wondering if perhaps you'd be more comfortable in regular music, instead of musical theater."

"Oh." I get it. So I wouldn't have to take Dance. Or Drama. Or hang with people who can just improvise armpit songs, because I'm a one-note wonder, not a triple threat. Got it. "But you recommended musical theater. You said if I wanted to do opera, I should learn all that stuff—acting and movement—to perform onstage."

"Well, it's certainly nice when an opera singer knows those things. But on the other hand, lots of singers are—"

"Big fat blobs who have to be wheeled across the stage on a handtruck?"

"I didn't say that." Rowena stops petting Fred, who looks at her reproachfully. "And you could never be that anyway."

"I was that."

"You were . . . chubby. In any case, I told her not to write you off so quickly in dance. I said I thought you were a young woman who could do anything she set her mind to—including dance."

I do Rowena's visualization exercise. I visualize myself dancing, flying across the stage, or part of a kick-line like a stupid Rockette.

It doesn't completely work.

"Do you think I can do it?" I mean the program, not just this song.

"I think sometimes it's good to go outside your comfort zone. On the other hand, I hate to see you lose track of who you are, just for the sake of trying to fit in," Rowena says.

"That's not what I'm doing. I just thought I'd like to try something different . . . for fun."

"Okay." Rowena reaches for the *Hairspray* music. "Well try it and see how it goes. For fun."

*A*re you sure?" Gigi squints at me, a lot like Fred the cat, while we're waiting to audition.

"Positive. My mom thought it was great."

"Like that's relevant."

Actually, what my mother—to whom I'm not currently speaking since the Arnold conversation—said was that the song I'd chosen was "a lot quieter than your usual stuff."

Gigi looks around at the growing group in the auditorium. "Rowena probably has copies of your regular music—I mean, if you change your mind at the last minute."

"I'm not changing my mind. Why do you care so much what I sing?"

"You're good at the opera stuff, Cait. Besides, I want you to get picked for the show because when—if—I get picked, we can go to practice together."

I look at her. Her hair's still pink, and if any of my old friends met her, they wouldn't understand why I hang with her. But I have this big urge to hug her. Instead, I say, "Don't worry. Maybe I'll surprise you."

"Hope so."

The accompanist starts playing the opening bars of "Good Morning, Baltimore." I may puke. I may actually puke right here, in front of a roomful of people. *What is wrong with me? What was I thinking?* I want to run. Hide, even.

But I start the first lines:

Oh, oh, oh, woke up today
Feeling the way I always do.
Oh, oh, oh, hungry for something that I can't eat
Then I hear the beat.

I look at the faces in the audience. They're frozen in fake smiles, sort of like in that one *Batman* movie when the Joker put chemicals in people's makeup that made them all look like him.

For the first time, I realize that:

1. The song requires a Broadway-belt voice, which I don't have.
2. The song requires me to move around (i.e., dance).
3. The girl who sang the song on Broadway was obese, wearing a bad wig and a hilarious costume. And, even though I feel that way sometimes, I don't actually weigh three hundred pounds.

I stare out at the audience—the people I've been trying soooo hard to impress the past few weeks—and for a minute, I wish I *was* really fat or ugly because that would give me a place to hide. They wouldn't laugh at me for being stupid and untalented then. They'd just ignore me like people ignore fatgirls. Being heavy makes it so much easier to sink through the floor.

I make an attempt at moving my feet and see Gigi bury her face in her hand.

I am such an idiot.

When I sit down, Gigi says, too quickly, "It wasn't that bad. It was good."

"Wow, I must have really sucked if you're lying to me like this."

Gigi shrugs. "It's over."

Behind me, Rex says, "I liked when you sang that opera thing better. You rocked at that."

I turn to look at him. I can't believe he said that. I can't believe anyone thought I rocked at *anything*.

"Yeah, I thought you did better with the opera too," another voice says.

It's Misty, sitting by Sean, her arm locked in his. That's when I realize she tricked me. She talked me into singing something I'd look stupid singing, so I wouldn't be any competition for her. She must have thought I rocked at opera too.

I start to say something, but then I accept: I only have myself to blame.

Subject: Unsurprisingly
Date: September 21
Time: 7:00 p.m.
Listening 2: Mad scene from Anna Bolena
Feeling: Miserable
Weight: 117 lbs. (and eating more cookies as I type this)

Don't ask, OK? OK, I tanked. They could go 2 battle w/ how bad I tanked. The problem is, everything I sing sounds like opera. And when you sing rock w/ an opera girl voice it's . . . . comical. ☹

The upside: I'll have a lot of free time since I'm not in the show. I can work on . . . . um, my relationship w/ Mom. Oh, and she'll be happy. She was already talking about rehearsals being 2 late before I even started @ the school.

The other upside: Misty wasn't very good either.

Gigi rocked, of course. I tried 2 look happy for her, but I kept thinking about what she said about wanting both of us 2 make it. She'll probably find other friends now that I'm not in the show.

Mom's out on a date w/ her married boyfriend, Arnold. She started bringing him home sometimes, but he always leaves by 10. Bet he tells his wife he's working late and she feels bad he has 2 work so hard. Boo-hoo. Wonder if he has kids.

*D*o you have kids?"

The question must surprise Arnold because his eyes don't immediately head for my chest, the way they usually do. But I'm wearing a sweatshirt.

"Oh . . . Cathy . . . I was just leaving. I thought you were in the house."

"I was getting something from the car." Actually, I've been waiting for him for the past half hour. But he didn't hear me go outside because he was busy at the time. ("Yeah. *Getting* busy," Gigi would say.) "So, do you?"

"Do I what?"

"Have kids?"

"Oh." Arnold still doesn't look at me. "No. I mean, I did, but they . . ."

"Died?"

He laughs. "No. They grew up. My daughter Alicia's at U.F. She's studying to be a music teacher. And my other daughter Melanie is in med school."

He looks at his car parked at the end of our driveway, probably trying to figure the odds if he made a run for it. He doesn't say any of the usual things adults say when they talk about their kids—like how his daughter would like me because we're both into music. He probably doesn't expect us to ever meet. The way I figure it is, best-case scenario, I end up with two steps who hate me because my evil mom stole their dad. Worst-case scenario: Mom gets dumped. Or maybe it'll be the other way around.

Arnold looks at his watch, then at the car again. "I have to go. It was nice talking to you, Cathy."

And he walks away —very quickly.

"Not just married," I tell Gigi the next day. "He has kids. Can you believe it?"

"Who?" We're standing in the hallway before school starts because Miss Davis said she'd put up the cast list this morning. Gigi's here to see what she's doing in the show. Me, I'm here for moral support. We've gotten a good spot near the front so people are pushing against us.

"Who?" I say. "Dr. Toe-Jam, that's who. Mom's boyfriend. He's married and has daughters in college—little Toe-Jams. Mom's a home-wrecker."

"Watch it!" Gigi elbows a guy who's pushing her. "Probably not. Usually men with a honey on the side never actually leave their wives."

"That's what Dear Abby says."

"Yeah, that's where I got it. Plus, my mom's guy dropped her like the proverbial potato when his wife found out. Your mom's guy probably will too."

"That's comforting."

"Well, maybe . . ."

But I don't get to hear the rest of Gigi's thought because that's when Miss Davis stumbles in, holding something that looks suspiciously like a cast list. You'd think a bunch of theater students would show more control than football players waiting for the starting lineup to be posted. You'd think that, but you'd be wrong. They rush at her shouting, "Miss Davis, did my number get chosen?" (She ignores this.) Since I know I didn't make it, I give up my spot by Gigi because I can give her moral support from a quiet corner near my locker. What was I thinking, singing that song? What possessed me? Did I not want to make it?

But I know what possessed me. Misty did. She wanted me to fail, but I was pretty clueless to go along with her.

And Misty, did she do something "jazzy" after telling me to? She did not. She sang "Popular" from *Wicked*, which would have been perfect from her, if only she could have sung it well. She did a duet with Sean too, and I tried to ignore the creeping tentacles of jealousy, reaching up my back.

The cluster around the cast list becomes a living thing, screaming and moaning. I start to slink off toward class.

"Caitlin!" Gigi's calling me from the screaming, jumping group.

"Catch you later!" I wave. I didn't realize I was upset until now. I'd rather wallow in private. I walk away. A hand grabs my wrist—a hand with black fingernails. Gigi. She drags me toward the mob around the cast list.

"Let go of me!" I protest. "I'm happy for you, but I've got—"

"Good news and bad news, girl."

She drags me through the subsiding crowd and places one black fingernail on the yellow page. I look at the spot where she's pointing. It says:

AN OPERATIC DUET TBA . . . . CAITLIN MCCOURT AND SEAN GRIFFIN

"Good news and bad news, girl," Gigi repeats.

Opera_Grrrl's Online Journal

Subject: Good News / Bad News—Again
Date: September 22
Time: 9:33 p.m.
Listening 2: Cecilia Bartoli, Mozart arias
Feeling: Surprised
Weight: 117 lbs.

The good news is: I get 2 sing in the show even though I tanked, tanked, tanked at audition. The bad news is: I have 2 sing w/ Sean.

   Explanation: I thought Sean was reeeeeeally nice (and cute!) when we 1st met. But ever since the day w/ La

Traviata, he hasn't even talked 2 me. He just hangs w/ his friends . . . . . . esp. the evil Barnacle Girl . . . . so I guess he doesn't think I'm as good as wonderful him. Oh, well.

When I saw Rowena, I asked her why—O, why—she put us together.

She let me know the faculty wasn't exactly thrilled w/ my audition (thx, Misty) but that she told them I'd done really well w/ La Traviata (!) "You 2 sound good together . . . . it'll be great."

Great. She gave me Sean's phone # and suggested I call 2 talk abt. our duet. I left a message on his ans. machine hours ago, and he hasn't called back.

Also on the upside (the 2nd good news, I guess): Misty didn't get a solo @ all! She has some solo lines in group #'s and that is IT!

I think I understand the term "poetic justice" now.

*T*he next day, Sean passes me a note in Davis's class.

Any ideas? Opera's not my "aria" of expertise (Haha)

The joke surprises me. So does his asking my advice. I write back:

Rigoletto?

The note comes back almost immediately:

Do I get to play a hunchback???

I write back:

Hunchback = Rigoletto = baritone. Duke of Mantua = tenor = you

Bummer! he writes back.

The Duke in *Rigoletto* is also a big jerk, so that sounds perfect for Sean.

After class, I stand outside waiting for Act Two with Sean. He shows up with, as usual, Misty hanging on him. I say, "Hey."

Misty keeps talking. "So unfair," she's saying. "They obviously knew who they were going to pick before the auditions. It's all favoritism."

I go through this little dream sequence in my head: I push her out of the way, she topples, propelled downward by her enormous chest, and can't get up but, instead, lies there, kicking like a cockroach on its back. And I say, "Excuse me? May I interrupt?"

In real life, I just say, "Excuse me? May I interrupt?"

Misty's face is all, *Please die!* but Sean says, "Catch you in class, Mist."

She stomps off. I stand there a minute, and when Sean doesn't say anything, I say, "Can we get together after school maybe? I have lots of CDs."

"Um, today's difficult."

"Tomorrow, then."

"No, not tomorrow either."

"Well, they're going to start rehearsals soon. Do you plan on being there?"

"When I have to."

"When you have to?"

He looks at me. "You know some people do have other responsibilities in life. We can't all be princesses."

"*Excuse* me?"

"Nothing. Forget I said anything."

But I heard him. My throat's all hardening up like it does when I'm about to cry. *Très* embarrassing. I try to say something else, I don't know what, something about how I am anything but a princess, or I just want to do what I'm supposed to, and what's up his butt that he acts like that's a bad thing, but I just walk away.

He follows me. *Don't follow me.* "Hey, look, I can't do it today. Why don't you bring your CDs tomorrow, and I'll try and listen to them if I get a chance?"

I don't look at him, because I don't want him to see how red my face is. I say, "If you get a chance?"

"Yeah. If I get a chance."

Unreal. I reach my History class. I stand there, and think for a minute, gulping a few times. That's when the bell starts to ring. I say, "If *I* get a chance, I'll bring them."

I don't know if he heard me, and I don't care.

 Opera_Grrrl's Online Journal

Subject: Un-Stinkin'-Real
Date: September 23
Time: 6:45 p.m.
Listening 2: Duets 2 Die For . . . . . . searching for a duet w/a great soprano part for me and a sucky tenor part for Sean
Feeling: Angry
Weight: Didn't weigh myself

Where does he get off calling *me* a princess? I'm sooo not a princess. Peyton & Ashley, maybe, but not me. Just b/c he's PO'd that he doesn't get 2 sing w/his fat girlfriend doesn't mean he has 2 take it out on me. What a SNOT!

After going through every CD I have, I call Rowena.

"What a coincidence. I just got off the phone with Sean about the same thing."

"With Sean?" Seems like I'm all about repeating other people today.

"Yeah, I'm so excited about you two performing together. He's such a nice boy too."

"Yeah." *If "nice boy" is adult-speak for a person who sucks up to teachers while terrorizing all others.* . . . "What did he say?"

"He was picking my brain for duet suggestions. I gave him a few."

Rowena is just about done telling me her duet ideas when Mom starts banging on the door. I keep talking. If Mom and I had struggled out of armed truce-land after school started, we went right back the day she admitted she knew Arnold was married. But finally, I get off the phone with Rowena and open the door.

"Thought maybe you wanted to go out to dinner," she says.

"We went out the other day."

Mom looks at the stereo, which is playing a track from *La Traviata.* "Actually, I didn't mean together. I thought maybe you'd like to take the car and see your friends. I'd give you money. You never see your friends anymore."

I have no friends.

The song on the CD ends, and I look at her. She's wearing a blue striped suit. Her hair is on top of her head, and her makeup's in natural skin tones.

"Oh." The next song starts. "He's coming over."

"Who? No, he isn't."

"I'm not stupid, you know. You want me out of the way, so you can be alone together." I sniff the air. Something's cooking—no Healthy Choice today—something with wine. I start to close the door. Around me, Violetta sings high A's. "Forget it."

She blocks the door. "At least turn off that racket when he gets here. And don't walk around in that outfit. It's obscene."

I look down. I'm wearing the same green leotard I had on the first day Dr. Toe-Jam got all pervy on me. "You don't have to worry about that. I'm not coming out."

But as soon as I hear Arnold at the door, I start feeling hungry. No, I am not just thinking about food to annoy Mom. I was really good at lunch today. I spent the entire time complaining about Sean instead of eating. Result: I'm starving. I turn down *La Traviata* so I can hear what Mom and Arnold are saying. I walk into the hall.

"So, your daughter's home," he asks.

"She's going out. We'll be alone."

"I knew I heard music. You said she's an opera singer, right?"

Mom told someone about my singing. *How weird.* She always acts like it's stupid. But she must think having an opera singer daughter makes her seem more classy. Or at least a little classy.

How sad.

Mom's talking now. "She must have left the CD player on."

I snap the music off in mid-song. Let her explain that one.

"I made my special coq au vin." Mom's voice is like a little song—the "Chicken Song." Since when is coq au vin her specialty? Microwaved Healthy Choice has always been her specialty when I'm around. My stomach gives a mighty growl that can probably be heard from the dining room. I decide I'm going in. I'm just going to nuke my Healthy Choice, come back in here, and eat it.

At the last minute, I decide to throw a T-shirt over my leotard, just so he can't look at my boobs.

"See, she's home!" Arnold declares, not too happily.

"What do you know?" Mom fake-smiles at me. "Caitlin, I thought you went out with your friends. Otherwise, I'd have set a place for you."

Unlikely. But I say, "That's okay. I was just getting a Healthy Choice. I'm on a diet."

Arnold's been standing since I came in, like he's ready to leave. "A diet? Pretty girl like you doesn't have an ounce to lose. Come sit with us. There's plenty."

"Oh, no thanks."

"The recipe really only makes enough for two, sweetheart," Mom says to Arnold. To me, she adds, "If I'd known you were dining at home, I'd have made more. Of course, we'd love to have you join us."

On the other hand, the chicken does smell good. "Well, maybe I'll just have a little bit then. I'll get a plate."

"I'll help you." Mom follows me. She closes the kitchen door and says, through clenched teeth, "What are you doing here?"

"Having dinner."

"But this was supposed to be our special time together, me and Arnold. If you crash our date, he'll think he's never going to be alone with me if we're together. Like I'm—"

"A mother?"

"Very funny. Do you know how hard it is to date when you have kids? Any time a man's interested, he gets a whole family."

I take out my silverware and drop it on the plate. "Well, obviously Arnold doesn't mind a family. He already has one of his own." I head for the dining room.

"Caitlin, so glad you decided to join us." Arnold spoons some chicken onto my plate.

"Well, it did smell good. Mom's an incredible cook."

"So tell me about your day, honey," Mom says, looking past me to Arnold.

But Arnold's still looking at me. "Did I hear *La Traviata* just now? I've always been a big opera fan."

"Really?" Surprise on surprise. My mother—who doesn't go to anything artsier than an Adam Sandler movie—is dating an opera fan.

"Oh, yes, we have season tickets."

We being him and his wife. I smirk at Mom.

She leans closer to Arnold. "More asparagus?"

"What? Oh, no, I'm fine. Everything's delicious." To prove it, he takes an enormous mouthful and turns to me, chewing. "That's from the final act, right?"

"Yes. It's my favorite opera." I'm loving that Mom's completely left out.

"Mine too. Have you seen it live?"

"Yes, my voice teacher took me. It was the first opera I ever saw."

"My first too. What a coincidence. Of course, that was when dinosaurs ruled the earth, but you never forget your first opera, do you?"

Mom's looking from her plate to Arnold and back, obviously trying to think of something to add. She knows I'll call her on it, if she says she goes to the opera, but there's nothing else to talk about. I'm screwing up my courage to pull a Gigi—to ask him if his *wife* loves opera too—when Mom says, "We should go sometime."

This should be beautiful. Mom's never been to the opera, so she doesn't know what it's like—all these rich people like Dr. and Mrs. Toe-Jam, seeing and being seen in jewels and tuxedos. A man could never go with his girlfriend. All his wife's friends would see him. I wait for Arnold to tell Mom it's impossible.

Mom's saying, "Caitlin always goes with her friends, but I love the music."

Right. I look at Arnold. *Okay, tell her. Tell her you can't take her.*

"What a great idea," he says. "I'd love to take you, Valerie. Nothing better than great music with a beautiful woman on my arm."

Mom beams at him. "You're so sweet." I stare. *Sweet. Right.*

"The season doesn't start until December," Arnold says, "but we'll definitely go."

Mom's smile widens when he says December, and I know what she's thinking—he's saying they'll still be together in December, that he'll blow his wife off. But me, I know he's lying to her. And, mad as I am at her for being a home-wrecker, I'm madder at Arnold because she's *not* wrecking his home. His home's fine. He's using my mother. And suddenly, even though Arnold looks completely stupid in sandals and socks, I realize he's not stupid at all. He's using her.

"Oh that would be wonderful," she's saying. "I'll buy a new dress."

"And we can have a fancy dinner before."

I look at the chicken on my plate and wonder how Arnold would look with sauce covering his bald head.

"Which opera is it?" Mom asks. "Hope it's a love story."

I push my plate away. "I'll let you two spend some time together."

"Oh, that's sweet of you, Caitlin," Mom coos. "Don't forget to clear your plate."

I take the plate into the kitchen and eat everything on it. Then I go to the back cupboard, where we keep the semisweet baking chocolate. I take it to my room and open it. It's white on the sides, and crumbles like a dog treat. I eat it anyway. I don't start the music. I don't want to sing anything he might hear.

It's like an opera, really. The other woman, the woman scorned. Except where Mom sees herself as Violetta, strong and in control of her men and her destiny, I see her as the doomed heroine of

Madame Butterfly—the beautiful geisha who thinks she's married a handsome American soldier for real, when really she's just a plaything while he happens to be in Japan, until he can go home and get a real American wife, and she's left there, singing *"Un bel di,"* one fine day, he'll come back.

I finish the chocolate and go to bed.

In the morning, I find an e-mail from an address I don't know. I open it.

> Subj: Duets
> Date: 9/24, 2:35 a.m., Eastern Standard Time
> To: Caitlinmcc@dslnet.com
> From: pippin725@micromail.net
>
> found these online
>   Sean
>   ps sorry I was a jerk

There's an attachment. I open it and find a list of eight soprano/tenor arias—two from Rowena's list, plus six others—and a link to an online classical music site.

I print out the list, but not the e-mail. Guys apologizing for being jerks is no new thing for me. Outside my door, I hear Mom singing around the house. Mom has a decent voice, but never sings unless she's really happy. Happy because of Arnold. I *so* can't deal with that now. I shower quickly and go out, taking my bicycle even though I know Mom will freak. I'll put my makeup on on the train, and Gigi will have to understand why I missed her. Maybe I can catch Sean at school.

♪ Opera_Grrrl's Online Journal

Subject: I Didn't Catch Sean @ School
Date: September 26
Time: 6:45 p.m.
Listening 2: "Con onor muore" ("Death w/Honor") from Madame Butterfly—the aria she sings as she commits suicide b/c she realizes the man she loves is just using her
Feeling: Sleepy
Weight: 118 lbs.

I didn't catch Sean @ school Thursday or Friday.
What I learned is:

1. Sean doesn't come 2 school early.
2. Sean doesn't stay late.
3. Sean doesn't sleep.

We finally chose our duet, "Parigi o cara" from La Traviata (a duet that always makes me cry b/c the lovers are singing about how they'll go 2 Paris 2gether & then—WHAMMO! She's dead. It also sort of makes me cry 2 think that Dr. Toe-Jam & I have the same favorite opera) entirely thru e-mails, which

Sean sends after 2 a.m. and I answer when I wake up at 5.

I also tried 2 tell Mom my whole theory about Dr. T-J & the opera and how he's lying 2 her if he says he's going 2 take her someplace so public. But she just gave me one of her you're-just-sooo-jealous-b/c-you-wish-you-were-cool-like-me looks and said, "Caitlin, you don't get it. December's a long time off. He's planning on *leaving* his wife by then. We'll be 2gether."

When I asked why he didn't just leave his wife now, she explained (slowly) that these things take time and we (we!) just had 2 be patient.

God! I'd puke but I'm trying not 2 eat.

I'm standing in the back of the Church by the Bay on Key Biscayne, where Sean works. After two weeks of rehearsing the group numbers and playing phone tag with Sean, I finally passed him a note Friday.

I KNOW it's a LONGShot, but do WE EVER get to SiNg iN the Same ROOM?

That's when he said maybe we could get together after his last church service. The choir's singing some tuneless hymn. I can hear Sean's voice over all the others. The minister says a final prayer, then invites everyone into the social hall for coffee and cake, sponsored by Mary Somebody in honor of Grandma Somebody's ninety-fifth birthday.

Mom and I used to go to church. She started, I *think*, as a way of making connections for real estate or meeting guys, neither of which worked. But it did get my mind off the fact that I wasn't visiting my father weekends, like every other divorced kid on the planet. Not that that bothered me or anything.

I see Sean gesturing from the choir area. Most people left for their refreshments, but Sean and one other guy stay back.

Sean introduces us. "Rudy, this is the girl I was telling you about—the singer."

I start a little. Sean told someone about me? I didn't think I was the slightest blip on his radar screen.

"Caitlin, this is Rudy Escobar. Rudy's the baritone section leader here."

"What's a section leader?" I say.

"Basically," Rudy says, "someone with a decent voice who sings loud enough to drown out all the old men in the choir."

"Rudy, that's not nice." But Sean's laughing.

"Sometimes the truth isn't pretty." Rudy touches my shoulder. "Oh, honey, before they hired Sean and me, the tenor and bass sections were to die *from*." He looks around to see if anyone's listening, even though he's talking at the top of his voice, which is loud. Real loud. "Half the men were mumbling into their music. The rest were singing "Shall We Gather at the River" like it was *The Flying Dutchman*."

Sean cracks up. The whole time Rudy's talking, I can't stop staring at him. He's a total bronze statue—tall, built, with brown skin and one of those short beards like professional opera singers wear. I don't usually go for the Latin lover type *or* guys with facial hair, but this guy's . . . um, everyone's type.

"Hello?" He passes a hand in front of my eyes. "Are you okay?"

Oh. *Excuse me while I die.*

I recover. "You know Wagner's operas?" I ask, remembering *The Flying Dutchman.* A brilliant save.

"Who doesn't?" He grins. "Baby, opera is my life. I was named Rudy—not after some *abuelo* but after Rodolfo in *Bohème.* My mama sung me to sleep with Mozart, and now—here I am—God's gift to the operatic stage."

"Which basically means he's a sophomore music student at U of M," Sean says.

"Only for now, Sean. In a few years, it'll be . . ." He gestures with his hands like there's a huge billboard behind us. "Rodolfo Escobar—live at the Met!"

I laugh. In my whole life I've never met a guy my age who knew anything about opera. Now, I'm in a room with two of them.

"Rudy said he'd play the piano for us," Sean says.

We start warming up, with Rudy playing exercises on the piano. He starts low and runs me higher and higher. When I reach a high D (the last *good* note I possess), he asks, "Can you do one more?"

"Only if you like screaming," I squeak.

"I bet you can. Want to try?"

I take a deep breath, think *up* like Rowena said, and go for E-flat.

Rudy stops playing. "Beautiful!"

"Didn't I tell you?" Sean says. "She's really something."

Rudy nods. "You're right. She's like "La Stupenda"—the great Sutherland."

Joan Sutherland was an opera singer before I was born. I can't believe he knows about her.

"Only with better teeth," Sean adds.

"Better everything," Rudy says. "Like Joan Sutherland if she was a hottie. You know you're a hottie, right?"

I actually giggle and forget that the scale said one hundred and sixteen this morning.

"Rudy, we're in a house of worship," Sean says.

Rudy claps his hand over his mouth. "Oops! Sister Mary Michael would so wash my mouth out with soap." He crosses himself.

I giggle again. I have this great thought. "Is everyone in college like you?"

"Like me, how?" Rudy exchanges a look with Sean. "Gifted and incredibly modest about it?"

"Like, do they know about opera and stuff?"

"Well, not the frat boys with the beer bongs, or the football team," Rudy says. "But the opera students are mostly like me. Only I'm the best, of course."

"Of course," Sean echoes.

"Wow," I say. "People I know don't know anything about art or music, and they think I'm weird because I do."

"You'll love college, girl," Rudy agrees. "I was so over high school. Even the so-called artsy people weren't into what I was. I'm trying to introduce Sean around, see about getting him some scholarship money for next year."

"I'll need it," Sean says.

Which gets me thinking. Worrying, actually. I've always figured I'd go to a college with a good music program like Indiana University or Oberlin (no way would Mom let me go someplace in New York City, but Indiana sounds so . . . wholesome). But I wonder if I'll need a scholarship too. We sure don't have extra money lying around. Mom's always said she'd make sure Dad pays, but I don't think he's actually required to pay for anything after I'm eighteen. So why would he? Because he *loves me* so much? Not likely. I push the thought back again.

Sean picks up our sheet music. "Shall we start?"

I'm grateful to be able to concentrate on singing. We sing really well together, and Rudy shouts, *"Brava!"* when we finish.

"Hey, don't you mean *bravi*?" Sean says. "For both of us?"

"Nope. I was just applauding her. Your head is swelled enough."

"Whatever." Sean looks at his watch. "Oh, gotta go. Family command performance."

"What else is new?" Rudy says. "Cut the cord."

"You're so sensitive," Sean says. We walk to the parking lot. I glance at my watch. We've been here over an hour, but it seems like ten minutes. I go for my bike.

"Need a ride?" Rudy asks.

I start to say I could use the exercise. Then I stop myself. Why *not* go with him? The guy's completely nice, and he must be safe

136

since he's Sean's friend. Not everyone's a stalker. And I met him at church. Not to mention his complete hotness. "Sure."

He loads my bike into the trunk of his old Camry and I give him directions. I want to ask him a million questions, about college, about opera. About Sean too. But I end up sitting there dead, stupid silent.

We're almost at my house when he says, "You hang with Sean much at school?"

"Not really. I was actually surprised when we got assigned to do a duet together. At school, he's always simulating sex with his girlfriend."

Rudy raises an eyebrow. "You mean Madame Misty? She's not his girlfriend."

"Could have fooled me."

"Nah, she's . . . not his type. He's mentioned you a lot, actually."

"Really?" This, together with the info that Sean isn't dating Misty, is incredible.

"Yeah. He thinks you're really talented."

"Oh."

I smile and try not to be disappointed. I mean, I want people to think I'm talented. Right?

"Do I have a college fund?"

Mom's in the living room, watching QVC. She glances up from the fire opal pendant they're displaying, but doesn't reply.

Okay. Let's try something else.

"Is Dad going to pay for college?"

Still nothing. The screen switches to a Dooney & Bourke bag. Mom leans forward and takes down a notepad to write down the info.

"Oh, god. So we have no plan?"

Mom looks away from the television. "Well, of course I have a plan, Caitlin. That's what I've been telling you. You think I don't worry about this stuff?" She looks back at the bag. Two hundred dollars.

I walk between her and the television. She can't buy two-hundred-dollar bags when I'm going to have to work as a singing waitress at Macaroni Grill after high school. "I missed the part where you told me."

She actually takes the remote and clicks off the TV. "With Arnold, baby. When I marry him, it will be like a built-in life—the house, the cars . . ."

"The man."

"Well, of course the man, Caitlin. But he'll help with your future."

"Do you love him?"

She doesn't answer right away, and I wonder what I hope she'll say. If she loves him, that's pathetic because he's using her. But if she doesn't love him and is screwing with his marriage, that makes her . . . can't say it.

"He's a sweet man, Caitlin. We'll have a good life with him."

It makes her a . . . I think about asking the question again, but I decide I don't want to know the answer.

"Who was that nice-looking young man I saw you with?" she says.

Typical. Let a hot guy drive me home and *that* she notices. "He's just a friend."

"Well, he was very . . . presentable. I was worried that everyone at that school was like that girl you brought home last week. The one with the . . . eyebrow ring."

I remember how Gigi described Mom: "Stepford wife without the husband."

"So I'm glad you've made some nice friends."

Not that you know anything about him, except that he's "presentable."

"Yeah, I'm glad too." I turn the TV back on, trading QVC for a way out of this conversation. She missed the purse—ha! I wait until she zombifies in front of the screen, then leave.

𝄞 Opera_Grrrl's Online Journal

Subject: Raised by Apes
Date: October 11
Time: 3:00 p.m.
Listening 2: La Traviata
Feeling: Happy
Weight: 116 lbs.

> Remember in the movie Tarzan when he doesn't think there are any other creatures like him . . . . then he meets Jane. That's how I feel today . . . . there are whole *departments* in universities where people actually "get" opera & don't think it's weird . . . . won't think *I'm* weird. I can't wait for college . . . . but I hope we can afford it w/out Arnold!!!

I'm on my mother's computer. QVC's still on in the living room, so I think it's safe. Mom has this program she uses for real estate, where you can get information about different properties—like look up an address and get the owner's name and how much they paid for it, or look up a person's name and find out where they live.

I type in MIKLOSHEVSKY, ARNOLD.

Three addresses come up. One's an office building near downtown. Another's a condo—probably an investment property. I know Mom would say it's good he has investments. The third is a house in Coral Gables, near where Dad lives.

I write that one down.

*I*n Drama, Gigi and I are doing this scene from *The Glass Menagerie*. Gigi plays Laura, a shy girl who's such a mess she can't even go to a typing class without puking on the floor. I play Amanda, Laura's witch of a mother, who lives in this dreamworld of the past where she was belle of the ball. She can't handle that she's stuck with no husband and a loser daughter.

Yes, I'm playing my mother. Miss Davis assigned the parts.

I definitely reek *less* at acting than dance (I mean, I can *speak*), but I still . . . well, suck. And I hate everything about Amanda, from her Southern accent (which I absolutely cannot do) to the all-too-familiar way she bullies her daughter. I'd never have chosen this scene. Even the lines are pretentious. Example: ". . . little bird-like women without any nest—eating the crust of humility . . ."

Like, hello? What does that mean?

So it's not a huge surprise when Miss Davis says, "No. That's not it at all."

"What's wrong with it?" Gigi says.

"This is a powerful scene," Miss Davis says. "A powerful example of an irresistible force meeting an immovable object. Amanda is motivated to make Laura change, and Laura is equally motivated to maintain the status quo. But it only works if each character's motivation is crystal clear." She turns to me. "How would you describe Amanda?"

"She's a complete . . . um, witch."

Giggles from the few people who weren't asleep.

"Would you care to elaborate?" Miss Davis says over them.

Not really.

I say, "She pushes her daughter around. She wants to run her life. She thinks she's really smart and comes up with schemes."

"Why?"

"Because she's . . . she wants to marry Laura off."

"Why?"

I think of Mom the other day, talking about marrying Arnold. "She wants Laura to marry some rich guy to support them."

"Why?"

Don't you know another word? "So she doesn't have to keep working or move in with their relatives. She doesn't care about Laura or think how hard it is for her to talk to people or do new things. She's completely selfish."

"But Amanda wouldn't see herself that way. Someone once said, 'A villain is the hero of his own story.' So you have to see Amanda's side. What is her side?"

I think about Mom, about how she rationalizes. "She'd

probably say she's doing it for Laura's own good. She wants Laura to be happy, and if Laura keeps being such a wuss, she's going to end up old and alone like . . ." I stop.

"Like her mother?"

I nod. "But Laura doesn't want those things. She wants to sit home and play with her glass animals. She wants to be alone."

"Does she really want that?"

"Yes. It would be so easy, only her mother doesn't care what Laura wants. She keeps talking about all the boyfriends she had when she was young, to show Laura she could get a man and Laura can't. She thinks Laura's a loser."

I'm not doing a very good job, seeing Amanda's side. But Miss Davis nods.

"Do you think Amanda ever had any dreams, Caitlin?"

But the bell rings, so I don't have to think about Amanda and her dreams. People run like rats from a sinking ship. Miss Davis says, "Okay, we're going to start rehearsing for the show in class, so we don't have any more time for scenes, but I think you girls should work on this on your own time. Friday, everyone come prepared to rehearse the first act finale."

Gigi elbows me on the way out. "Our *own* time. Like we have all this free time."

"She's doing it for our own good."

We break into unreasonable laughter.

Gigi's number (*one of* her numbers) is a duet with Sylvanie, a tribute to Judy Garland, who did movie musicals in the 1940s. So now, we sit with Sylvanie and her friends in the cafeteria, or some-times go to The Pit, where I try to avoid GrandMa's cookies. I thought it would be weird sitting with them, like when I started dating Nick and sitting with his friends at lunch. We didn't have anything to talk about. But now I know that when you're in a show with people, you can talk about the show . . . endlessly.

Except today, Gigi's talking about what I'm eating. My new plan (after the baking chocolate incident) is to bring a nutritious lunch from home—like a sandwich on pita bread—and a bottle of water. Maybe the reason I'm pigging out is I'm not letting myself eat enough. Anyway, I've been doing it for a few days now, and I'm down to 113.

"That's all you're eating?" Gigi says.

"My jeans are tight."

"Well, yeah, Caitlin. That's because they're a size zero."

I think of Peyton and Ashley. "They're a two."

"There's a difference?"

"There's a huge difference. Like ten pounds."

Gigi rolls her eyes. "I think you could do at least a size three without the marching band playing the 'Baby Elephant Walk' when you walk along the sidelines."

Of course this school doesn't have a marching band, much less sidelines.

"I wear a seven," she says. "Am I fat?"

Of course she's not fat. But she's also tall. I never notice anyone else's fat.

"Caitlin thinks I'm fat," Gigi announces, pouting.

"Girl, you're way too fixated on weight," Sylvanie says.

"I didn't say she was fat!"

"No, but you're always sitting here with your celery," Sylvanie says. "Makes me feel like eating more, just watching you."

I take a bite of my sandwich and look at them like, *Happy?* I try to chew real slow to make it last longer. Peyton and Ashley could take an hour to eat a side salad. "Can we talk about something else? Please?"

"So, are you, like, singing opera in the show?" Sylvanie says.

"Um, yeah. I have a duet." I glance over to where Misty's sitting, assuming Sean's there too. He isn't. It's Wednesday and we haven't practiced since Sunday.

"You have the prettiest voice," Sylvanie says. "I wish I had a voice like yours."

"Thanks." I figure she's just being nice, to make up. Sylvanie's like Gigi—one of those people who's good at everything so she can afford to be kind to mere mortals. Two weeks into rehearsals, my screw-ups in dance are legendary. She probably feels sorry for me.

But Gus's sidekick, Rex says, "How high can you go with that thing? Can you break glass?" He holds up his watch, a digital one.

"Not that glass. It's plastic. I hit an E-flat the other day, though. A high one."

"Prove it," Gus says.

"Nope." I learned early—and the hard way—that people may

say they want to hear you sing in public places, but if you actually do it, they'll think you're tremendously weird. Nick told me that, actually, but even Nick could be right sometimes.

"Please," Gus says.

"Please," Rex repeats. "I think I'm in love with you."

I laugh and shake my head. "No way. You'll have to wait until dress rehearsal." Then in case they think I'm being a snob, I say, "Okay, so how bad did we suck today in Drama?" Because I also learned early on that if you're good, people think you're a snob, and the best way to keep that from happening is to put yourself down.

And it works.

"You were fine," Rex says. "Davis doesn't appreciate brilliance. I mean, she gave me a C on my scene."

"The *noive*!" Gigi says.

And then everyone starts talking about how mean Miss Davis is, and, for the first time since I've been here, I feel like maybe, just maybe, I'm not the weirdest person around.

Subj: Practicing
Date: 10/14, 10:35 p.m., Eastern Standard Time
To: pippin725@micromail.net
From: Caitlinmcc@dslnet.com

It was fun practicing the other day. Don't you think we should get 2gether again sometime? There's no rehearsal tomorrow.

It took me an hour to compose that e-mail, so I don't sound like I'm nagging or stalking him or anything. And then I saved it in *Mail Waiting to Be Sent* for another two before I decided to go for it.

The next morning, there's a reply.

Subj: Practicing
Date: 10/15, 2:03 a.m., Eastern Standard Time
To: Caitlinmcc@dslnet.com
From: pippin725@micromail.net

we could do it 2morrow (actually 2day) if you don't mind coming here.

I can't do my homework if you're going to scream like that!" I'm in Sean's actual room in Sean's actual apartment. The voice comes from the kitchen. "Learn to appreciate great music!" Sean yells back.

"You call that music?" says the voice from the kitchen.

It's after six, and we barely started singing. It took ninety minutes to get here from school—an hour to drive here, and another half hour to pick up Sean's sister, Desi, from aftercare. Then it took another half hour to get Desi started doing her homework. Now she's stopped again.

"Can you come help me?" she asks.

From Sean's bedroom window I see a guy working on an old Toyota, and a group of boys playing basketball with a hoop made from a milk crate. The place looks like the type of apartment complex you live in if your dad stops paying child support. For the first time ever, I appreciate my dad. Well, maybe just for a second.

"No, I can't help you," Sean says. "I'm trying to sing."

"*Trying* is right," his sister says. "I need heelllllppp!"

What I do appreciate is Sean. I've figured out why Sean never hangs around after school. He doesn't have time. I don't even know when he practices for himself.

"Why don't you warm up," he tells me. "I'll be back in a second."

I sing some warm-ups, trying not to listen. I look at the walls. Every inch is covered with murals. Behind me, refugees arrive on a boat made from an old car. To my left, the Space Shuttle breaks up, shattered pictures of astronauts raining to the ground. Sean explained that his father's an artist "in his spare time," but mostly he paints houses.

When Sean gets back, I say, "It's nice that you help her so much."

"Nah, it's not nice. She's my sister." He heads for the keyboard in the corner of the room and sings, "Step to the keyboard, my dear."

"You do that too?" I say.

"What?"

"Sing things. Like you're in an opera."

"Sure. Doesn't everyone?"

I shake my head. "No one *I* know."

"You know me." He gestures to the keyboard. "Now warm up."

I continue, but the whole time he's playing exercises, I'm so worried about impressing him that I can barely sing. Finally, he stops playing. "You're really tense." He starts massaging my neck, kneading the muscles. "Roll your head back." His hands are really strong, stronger than he looks, and I find myself relaxing, like I could fall asleep in his arms.

"Mmm . . . that feels good," I say.

"I used to live with my mom. She typed all day, and she'd come home all tense. So she taught me to give her neck rubs from an early age. If this singing thing doesn't work out, I'll be a masseur."

"How long did you live with your mother?"

"Until I was ten. Then she left." He stops rubbing my neck. "Okay, ready?"

"Thanks." I nod. I want to ask him more about his mother, but I don't think he wants me to. So I say, "Yeah, let's do it."

We go through the song five times. It's tough going at first because I'm still—let's admit this—thinking about what it was like to have Sean's hands on my neck. *What is wrong with me?* But finally I get a grip and get through it a couple of times decently.

"Good," Sean says. "Want to call it quits—end on a high note?"

"Sure," I say. "You were good too."

"Thanks." He looks at me. "You're not like I thought you were."

"What?"

He shakes his head. "Sorry. It's just . . . I really didn't want to bring you here today. That's why I've been avoiding practicing together."

"What do you mean?"

"Nothing. It's just . . . I thought you were kind of a snob, but you're not, are you?"

"No." *Is he kidding?* "You thought *I* was snobby?"

"I wasn't sure. You seemed nice at auditions, sort of shy. But then I saw you at Wendy's that time, with those friends of yours, and after that, you barely looked at me. So I figured, Okay, the girl's a homecoming queen from hell." He shrugs. "Sorry."

"Thanks a lot." But I remember that day at Wendy's, Peyton and Ashley, laughing at Sean. I hope he didn't see them, but I bet he did. I want to think of a way to explain it away, but I can't. "I'm not really friends with those girls."

It's my way of apologizing. Sean nods.

"I thought you weren't talking to me because I'm not as good as you," I say.

"Really?" He looks confused. "No way. You're incredible."

I smile at that but say, "You were hanging with Misty all the time, and she's . . . scary. You never talked to me. So I figured you had enough friends."

"Misty and I . . . we drifted apart." He makes a drifting gesture with his hand.

"In the past week?" *Stupid!*

"Yeah. It had something to do with her saying she talked you into singing that dumb song at auditions."

"It wasn't *that* dumb," I say.

"Yeah, it was," he says.

"Okay. It was. But what does that have to do with you?"

"She was laughing about it, about how stupid she thought you looked. I just thought it was a really bitchy thing to do."

"Mm-hmm." I nod and turn away, so he can't see me blushing.

"Anyway, we're not *enemies* or anything. I just decided I needed other friends."

"So you two were just friends?"

"Yeah, what else?"

"Hey, I don't hear any singing in there!" Desi's voice comes from the living room. "Are you guys . . . kissing or something?"

I feel my face heat up, and I look away from Sean. He says, "We're caught."

"Let's sing it again," I say. I'm in no hurry to get home. It's a Tuesday, a probable Arnold night. I'd much rather stay here awhile.

𝄞 Opera_Grrrl's Online Journal

Subject: Noises I Can Hear, Sitting in My Bedroom
Date: October 15
Time: 10:45 p.m.
Listening 2: See below
Feeling: Distressed
Weight: 113 lbs.

· Arnold's car in the driveway
· Front door, opening & closing
· Giggling (Mom)

- Nerdy laugh (him)
- Her, asking if he'd like coffee (she doesn't know how 2 *make* coffee. She buys it at Starbucks)
- Him, turning down coffee (like she must have known he would)
- Her bedroom door, opening
- Her bedroom door, closing
- Silence
- Silence
- Silence (If I listened closer, I bet I could hear something. But I don't want 2)
- The 1st act of La Bohème on my headphones
- Her bedroom door, opening
- The front door, opening
- The front door, closing
- Arnold's car, pulling out of the driveway
- Her bedroom door, closing
- The 2nd act of La Bohème, on my headphones

*I*n *Bohème*, Rodolfo loved Mimi. He was happy to hold her cold little hand, to light her candle, and stand in the dark, watching it flicker. Are there any guys like that in real life? Or is that why in the best operas, someone dies in the end? Because if they lived, they'd figure out that it's not for real.

I watch Arnold's taillights fade down the street and listen to *Bohème*. Musetta sings about how her beauty drives men mad. I know these characters better than I know anyone real.

I wish I was still at Sean's apartment, singing "*Parigi o cara.*" Even helping Desi with her homework would be fun. I ended up staying another two hours and eating ramen noodles with them. I think about calling Sean. I know he's awake. He's always up late, judging from his e-mails. But it would be too weird to dump all my crap on him. We've only been friends a week.

I go online. I was going to write in my journal, but I start an e-mail instead.

Subj: Can't sleep
Date: 10/15, 11:09 p.m., Eastern Standard Time
To: pippin725@micromail.net
From: Caitlinmcc@dslnet.com

I lied when I said I wasn't friends w/those 2 girls. I *was* friends w/them before . . . . . but now I see that they just made me feel bad about myself . . . . like I have 2 be on my best behavior around them & have my makeup & hair perfect & pull in my stomach & not eat 2 much . . . . and def. NOT SING OPERA!!! They make me feel like my mother does . . . . I don't know who I really am . . . . when I was w/u 2day was 1 of the 1st times in a long time I didn't feel like I was trying 2 be some1 else. Not 2 much anyway . . . . . .

I can't send that to him. It's an atrocity. I delete it and start another one. I try to make it sound casual, spending five minutes coming up with an opera aria title that will fit the subject line—"*Questa o quella.*" This or that. I hope he gets it. I don't know what to write, that will let him know I like him, without letting him know I LIKE HIM.

Subj: Questa o quella
Date: 10/15, 11:35 p.m., Eastern Standard Time
To: pippin725@micromail.net
From: Caitlinmcc@dslnet.com

Did Desi *ever* finish her homework? Will she get in trouble if she doesn't? Will you? Thanks for helping me w/the song. Do you think we'll be good 2gether (singing, I mean)? I'm listening 2 Bohème now. I wish I could go 2 Paris. I wish I was in Paris now, in a garret, w/a candle . . . . Caitlin

I hit send before I can change my mind. I go to bed. The third act of *Bohème* begins on my headphones. Mimi's death scene. I don't fall asleep until it's over. I cry. I always cry.

The next morning, there's an e-mail from Sean.

Subj: Re: Questa o quella
Date: 10/16, 3:05 a.m., Eastern Standard Time
To: Caitlinmcc@dslnet.com
From: pippin725@micromail.net

Great subject line (I had 2 look it up online 2 know what it meant)! Desi did finish. I might have accidentally done some for her, but I used my left hand so it looks authentic. Going 2 bed now—gotta get my full 2 hrs. sleep. Paris sounds good 2 me 2. Maybe we'll sing there someday☺ WE WILL BE GREAT (SINGING) TOGETHER!!! *YAWN* S

Subject: Sean
Date: October 29
Time: 10:45 p.m.
Listening 2: "L'amour est un oiseau" ("Love Is a Bird")
from Carmen
Feeling: Busy
Weight: 114 lbs.

Sean and I have been hanging out 2gether the past 2 weeks. A lot. Most days after school, we have rehearsals. But at least 1x a week, I go home w/Sean, help Desi w/her homework (a thankless task), practice, then eat ramen noodles & sometimes watch his dad, "Griff," paint the walls. We always go 2 his house, but 2day after rehearsal, he said maybe we could practice at my place, since it's closer.

I must have had a look on my face . . . . a look that said I'd rather have honey dripped on my eyes & be placed in an ant farm than have him come over b/c he raised an eyebrow and said, "I understand."

But the look on his face was like, I understand you don't want me 2 meet your mother . . . . . . so I said he didn't understand. I didn't want him 2 meet my mother b/c I didn't want him 2 meet *her*, not the other way around.

Then I wanted 2 push the words back. He'd probably think I was a freak. But he nodded and said, "OK, my place it is."

But on the way 2 his house, he told me about his own mom.

Griff, turns out, is Sean's mother's 2nd husband. She had Sean w/ the 1st one, Desi w/ some guy she met @ a party. Then she married Griff.

Sean says they were happy for *maybe* a year. Then his mom started not coming home nights. Even at 9, Sean knew what was up. Then 1 day, her things were gone. Griff told them, "It's OK, dudes. You can hang w/ me until she gets back." That was 8 yrs. ago.

Sean says they're happy, but he wonders if Griff could be a real artist instead of just a housepainter, if he didn't have them around. So that's why he tries 2 be superhuman, taking care of Desi, helping around the house, & doing every1's home-work. He wants 2 get a scholarship 2 U of M so he can go 2 school for free and still take care of Desi.

Sean says he thinks his crappy life has been a good thing because it's taught him the tenacity (which means "persistent determination." I looked it up) he needs 2 make it in the arts. "Some people aren't willing 2 struggle," he said. "They might quit the 1st time they have 2 wait tables. Me, I'm used 2 sur-viving."

Wow. So after he was done, I told him the whole story of my life w/ Mom and non-Dad (but not abt. Arnold!!!). No compari-son 2 his. I mean, *my* mom's not *on* anything. She's just incredibly annoying. He said he bets I'm tenacious 2, since I've gotten 2 be really good w/o anyone encouraging me.

Maybe he's right. I haven't talked 2 my friends from Key in a long time . . . . I've been telling myself it's b/c I don't have time with rehearsals and everything, but it's not just that. I've changed. I'm no longer Caitlin McCourt, mild-mannered cheerleader wannabe. Like Clark Kent or Bruce Wayne, I now have a stronger alter ego. I am Opera_Grrrl, defender of all things operatic!

*T*here's no school because it's a "teacher planning" day, so I'm sitting at Gigi's house. I'm helping her dye her hair. Miss Davis told her she had to choose a color a little "closer to nature" for the performance. We're dying it Light Spice—a reddish brown, and we're channel surfing. Gigi stops at this morning show where a girl about our age is talking about how she got pregnant.

"There's just three guys it could be," she's saying.

Gigi snorts. "Just three!"

"Shh. I want to hear this. Have some respect for the pregnant."

"And one's a one-night stand," the TV girl continues. "He won't support me."

Gigi rolls her eyes. "Big surprise."

"Shut up! Shut up!"

"I'm not sure I'm ready to be a mother," the TV girl says.

Gigi starts to make another crack, but then looks at me and

gets quiet. She waits until the show cuts to a commercial and then says, "Let's make popcorn."

"We just ate," I say, not getting up. "It's ten-thirty, and we had bagels before we went to Walgreen's for the hair dye."

"Pleeeeze, Cait, I'm *starving*. Humans actually *need* calories to sustain life."

"Okay, but I'm not eating any." I follow her into the kitchen. While the popcorn pops, I say, "Do you think people on those morning shows are for real?"

"Sure. Why not?" she says.

"I hear a lot of them are aspiring actresses."

"We should go on one then—you and me—when we're in New York trying to make it." She checks out her reflection in the door of the microwave. "This is gonna look *soooo* totally lame."

"It'll look fine. What would the show be about—the one we're going on?"

"*I was a Teenage Pageant Queen,*" Gigi says.

"No. *I Was a Drama School Dropout.*"

"No, wait. I have the perfect one for you," Gigi says. "*My Mother Won't Stop Dressing Like Me!*"

"Hey, watch it."

"You're just mad you didn't think of it first."

"Am not." I glance at the microwave clock. "Be quiet. We have to listen to the popcorn now."

So we stand there listening to the pops, inhaling the smell. When the pops slow down to five seconds between them, we take the bag out of the microwave. I reach for it.

"Thought you weren't having any."

I stick my tongue out at her.

"What's the Toe-Jam update?" she asks.

"She still thinks they're getting married."

"Are they?"

"He's still with his wife."

"I wonder what she's like."

"I don't know. I looked up his address on the computer."

"Really? You know where his house is? Have you gone there?"
Gigi asks.

"Too chicken."

That's all Gigi needs to hear. As soon as she washes out the
hair dye (she looks really pretty, but I don't mention it since I
know she's not happy about looking so conventional), we're in her
mom's car heading there.

The house is an ordinary, very nice house like Dad's. But one
thing I notice is there's a yellow Lab in the backyard. I always
wanted a yellow Lab. I used to ask Mom for a dog every year for
Christmas. ("Dogs are creatures that eat their own puke, Caitlin,"
she told me.) What I wonder now is, *Is it Arnold's kids' dog? Did
he get it for them for Christmas or Hanukah or whatever they cele-
brate?*

"Nice place," Gigi says.

"Yeah." I chew my cuticle. "Can we leave now?"

Subject: The Kind of Thing I Love About This School
Date: November 2
Time: 8:14 p.m.
Listening 2: "The Lullabye of Broadway" (finale 4 our show)
Feeling: Amused
Weight: 115 lbs.

In English class we're reading this book called Stargirl, which is basically abt. embracing non-conformity (like people at this school need a lesson in *THAT!*). The whole grade is reading it. Anyway, 2day the principal, Mr. Cirrone, actually came 2 school *dressed* as Stargirl, wearing a wig and a long prairie dress, and carrying a ukulele. In my old school, people would have def. thought that was très lame, but here they thought it was funny.

One of the group numbers in *Welcome to New York* is "Christmas Bells" from the musical *Rent*. That's good because there's no dancing but bad because it's a rock opera. I started out playing a homeless person, but Miss Davis said my voice stuck out too much on the high parts (Story of my life), so I got switched to playing a junkie, belting out, "Got any X, any smack, any horse?" My mom would be so proud. I haven't even told her the performance dates yet. Gigi's a junkie too, and Sean has one of the leads and stands near us. We listen to Gus and Rex, who play two gay lovers, making homophobic comments. I start to whisper something to Gigi, but she isn't paying any attention to me.

"What are you staring at?" I say.

"Would you just look at that?" She gestures at Gus.

"What?" But I think I know. Gus has on these tight sweatpants which make, um, certain things very . . . and I mean *very* apparent.

"Someone should tell him to buy a jockstrap," Gigi comments.

"Oh, okay, why don't you tell him?" I joke, before I realize that she might actually do it.

Gigi nudges Sylvanie, and Sylvanie nudges the girl by her, and soon, we're all pretty much staring at Gus's crotch. In fact, we do it any time Miss Davis yells *"cut!"*

"We should give it a name if we're going to talk about it so much," Gigi says.

"Woody?" Sylvanie suggests.

I say, "There was a comic who used to call his thing Mr. Happy. Maybe we should call Gus's Happy?"

"How about Doc?" Gigi suggests.

"Definitely not Bashful," I say, and everyone laughs.

My mouth's still moving when Miss Davis notices us. "Ladies and gentlemen, you are drug addicts in desperate need of a fix. No giggling."

Which sends us diving to cover our mouths with our hands. Except Misty, who isn't in on the joke. She says, "I think that's very unprofessional."

You would. Misty's playing a homeless person. When I got sent to the junkies, she got my solo line. Oh, well. I'm happy to stand with my friends.

When Miss Davis looks away, Gigi whispers, "Happy it is. Pass it on."

The last group number is in the "classic Broadway" section of the show. It's from *A Chorus Line*, and it's all dancing. After a few rehearsals, Ms. Wolfe says maybe the non-dancers can sing by the side of the stage. I pretend not to know she means me. I am *not* dancing by the side of the stage with this girl Anastasia who weighs over two hundred pounds and got a doctor's note to get out of Dance because she doesn't want to wear a leotard. I can do this.

When I tell Sean this after rehearsal, he says, "Of course you can."

"Oh, of course," I say. "I'm a legendary talent in dancing."

"I can work with you. Our duet's coming along. Maybe if you'd deign to let me go to your house Sunday after church, we could go over the steps."

"Really? You'd do that?" I feel like busting a cheerleader move, and I tell myself it's because I'm excited about getting some dance help, but I know it's really because I'm excited about seeing Sean on a weekend. We've become really good friends, but I wonder if I want it to be more than that.

That night after rehearsal, I'm in my bedroom. Mom's not home, and I've been Googling opera trivia. I found this cool website about the opera legend Maria Callas. I want to send Sean the link, but he hasn't answered my last e-mail, and there's a limit to how many e-mails you can send a guy without looking stalker-ish. I log off so I won't send it, even though I know I'll be back on in five minutes.

Other than Sean, my e-mail box has been pretty much empty. I never hear from my old friends. I don't know why that bothers me. What's the use of outgrowing people if they don't even notice you've outgrown them?

But the phone rings. It's Sean. "Hey, I just got home and I thought I'd call you."

"Cool. I found this really cool Maria Callas site. I'll send you a link."

We talk awhile, me wracking my brain trying to think of stuff to say so he won't hang up. But finally, it's time, and that's when he says it:

"Love you."

What? But I heard him. I remind myself that *love you* (or was it even *love ya?*) isn't *I love you.* Not at all. I shouldn't read too much into it, like in that Tom Cruise movie where all the girls are talking about how he says *Love ya* when he can't commit.

So I say, "Love you too," trying for the exact same inflection.

Then I hang up.

♪ Opera_Grrrl's Online Journal

Subject: Love Ya
Date: November 3
Time: 11:13 p.m.
Listening 2: "Che gelida manina" (hallway scene from La Bohème)
Feeling: Tired
Weight: 115 lbs.

Or was it, I love you?

ot coincidentally, I scheduled Sean's visit for 11:30, on Sunday. Mom's open houses are usually at noon, but she goes early to make sure the homeowners cleaned up and didn't leave anything tacky lying around, like black velvet Elvis paintings. (She says she throws the extra junk in the garbage can.) Coast should be clear by eleven-ish.

But at 11:15 she's still home. At 11:25 I go to investigate. She's in her room wearing a pink thong bikini and full makeup.

I say, "Have open houses gotten a lot more casual lately?"

Inside, I'm panicking. Panicking, I tell you.

"Oh, darn client decided not to sell—after I told another client I couldn't take her around. Can you believe that? So I have a free Sunday for once. I'm catching some rays."

"At the beach?" I ask, hopefully.

"Nah, just outside. I have a client at three. Want to join me?" She looks at my legs. "You've gotten pasty since you started that arts school."

"Um, no." If she goes out right now, I can sneak Sean past her. I pick up the suntan lotion. "Here you go."

"I'll put it on in here, let it sink in. UV rays can destroy the skin, Caitlin."

"I know, I know." *Get her outside.* "Here, I'll do your back."

Three skin preparations later, she's out the door. I didn't have to worry, though. Sean's late. At 12:15 the phone rings. I pounce on it.

"Hey, my mom let me borrow the car. Want to hit the beach?"

It's Gigi. I glance at the clock. If Sean's coming, I should wait. But what if he forgot and I'm stuck here, with Valerie, the Hawaiian Tropic babe?

"Caitlin, if you don't want to go, just say so. I'm a big girl."

"It's just . . . Sean's supposed to come over."

"He blew you off?"

"Not necessarily."

"Don't move. I'm coming over." She hangs up and doesn't answer when I call back . . . repeatedly.

It's almost 12:45 when she shows up, giving a confused glance at Harold the flamingo, who's dressed like a pilgrim now. Still no Sean. "Well, screw him," she says.

"Right. I'll get my suit on." I go to put on my bathing suit, a tank. I own bikinis, but I sort of hate having people look at my body. Nick used to tell me to wear a T-shirt over my suit because I looked fat. Now I realize he just didn't want other guys looking at me—another level of his BS. I was skinny. Today I look in the mirror. I weigh one hundred and sixteen now, eleven pounds more than I weighed when I left fat camp last summer. I haven't binged since that night with the baking chocolate, and I'm keeping away from the cookies . . . mostly. Now I survey my body. One-sixteen isn't as heavy as I thought. It's fat in Ashley-land, or if you're Mom. I don't wear a size zero, but I bet if I ate normal meals, I could maintain this, no problem. And I look good. Normal good.

I put on a bikini, but I put a long T-shirt over it for some added coverage.

"What?" Gigi says when I come out. "Not a thong like Momzilla?" She gestures toward Mom, who's in the yard giving a full moon to the world.

"Please die," I tell her. I head to the kitchen to get some Diet Cokes.

Of course that's when the doorbell rings.

I try to run in before Gigi opens it, but I'm too late. Next thing I know, Gigi's saying, "Caitlin gave up on you an hour ago." I look out and see Sean and Rudy. Gigi checks Rudy out. "Who are you?"

"He's a friend of Sean's." I'm trying to usher them . . . somewhere, but it doesn't work because Gigi's going to the beach while Sean and Rudy are heading to my room to practice dance steps. So the next thing I know, Mom's sweeping in from the yard.

Worlds . . . colliding . . . Duck! Take cover!

"Caitlin," she says. "Did you throw a party and not invite me?"

Of course she comes in when any guys show up. And of course she didn't put on a cover-up. And of course she's wearing high-heeled sandals, the better to flex her butt muscles. In fact, the living room is quite full with me, Gigi, the guys, and Mom's butt.

"Um, no. We were just leaving . . . for the beach."

I say this even though it's fairly obvious we're not *all* going to the beach. Rudy and Sean are dressed for church. But I have to get them out of the house before Mom—

"You haven't introduced me to your friends."

Too late! Mom's advancing on Rudy. "You're the nice young man who drove Caitlin home a few weeks back."

Gigi raises an eyebrow, Rudy backs away, and Sean attempts, "Nice to meet you, Mrs. McCourt."

"Call me Valerie. Mrs. McCourt sounds like a teacher."

I find my voice. "Mom, you know Gigi." I wait for her to make eye contact. "And this is Sean and Rudy. We were just leaving." I hand Sean the cooler.

He gets the hint and leaves. Gigi and Rudy follow, then Mom says, "You're welcome to stay here. I could make sandwiches."

"No, that's fine, Mom."

So we go to the beach. It turns out that Sean, who practically lives out of his car, has swim trunks with him, and Rudy rolls up his pants. We stop at Mr. Pizza and order one to go. Then we head to Bill Baggs Park and choose a spot near the lighthouse. I used to come here all the time with my friends from Key, but it's been a while.

"You should come to Choral Camp this summer," Rudy tells Gigi and me. "It's at the University of Miami, and they're already planning for it. I'm going to lead a small ensemble group. So of course I'm trying to recruit good people so my group will be the best. Sean's already coming. I assume you're brilliant too."

"Good assumption." Gigi smiles.

"Rudy knows everything about opera," I tell Gigi.

"I guess someone has to," she says.

I kick some sand at her, then freeze. Walking about five feet away from me are all—and I mean *all*—my old friends from Key, including Nick. Three football players, two cheerleaders, and a partridge in a pear tree.

Omigod. I'm in ex-boyfriend hell. I wish I'd left the T-shirt on. I suck in my stomach.

Saint, the guy I dated after Nick, is carrying a cooler that I know is filled with beer (hidden under the Coke cans). "Hey, Caitlin," he says.

Can't talk. Dying. "Hey."

They reach our blanket where they salaam like extras in a production of *Turandot* and I introduce them to my friends.

"I remember you from Wendy's," Ashley says to Sean. "Nice bathing suit."

Sean doesn't put down his pizza, but salutes. Finally, the only one left is Nick. I'm holding my pizza *and* my breath, wondering what he's going to say. But he just nods and trudges along after them. I watch, frozen, until he's about ten feet away.

"Who's that?" Sean says.

"Who?" I say.

"Mr. Intensity with the green eyes."

"Oh." I pull my own gaze away from Nick. "My ex."

Sean glances in Nick's direction, and at that moment, Nick looks back. When he sees Sean watching him, he looks away.

"Why'd you break up?" Sean asks.

I use my pizza crust as a pencil, writing my name in the sand, trying to think of the right answer, the good lie, like *We drifted apart* or *We wanted to see other people.* Yeah. That one's good. I draw a heart around my name. Nick's about fifteen feet away and the sound of the surf is hard in my ears.

"He beat me up," I say.

Way to kill a party, Cait. Sean's mouth makes a surprised O. Everyone's does. Gigi looks like she wants to say something, but for once she's speechless. In fact, the world goes eerily silent, except the rock and roll of the ocean, and I remember sitting on this beach with Nick, less than a year ago, by the shadow of the lighthouse. The beach hasn't changed, just me. Why, why did I tell them, especially Sean? I want this guy to like me, so I let him see me as a victim? The wind hits my eyes, and I look at Nick. He doesn't look back. I feel my eyes start to tear up. "Now you all think I'm really stupid."

That's when Sean reaches for me, first one arm, then the other. He pulls me to him. He feels warm and safe, and no one says a thing for a minute.

I break the silence. "It's not that big a deal."

"It sure is. No one should treat you like that." Sean looks after Nick. "What a jerk. Why do guys do stuff like that?"

I shrug. "He had a rough childhood, I guess."

Gigi makes a noise, and Sean says, "*I* had a rough childhood. That's no excuse. That's just dumb." He looks at me. "Sorry. It's not you I'm mad at."

"I know," I say, though I don't. Not really. "I guess I used to make excuses for him."

Sean frowns. "Well, I'm glad you stopped. You don't need that guy. You don't need anyone."

"Hey," Rudy says. "Anyone want my pepperoni?" He holds a handful out.

"Eww, no thanks," Gigi says.

"I'll take it." Sean releases me to take it.

"I knew you would," Rudy says. "A human garbage disposal."

We stay there the rest of the afternoon until, finally, Sean says he has to go home to help Desi make the solar system out of fruit for school. The whole time I can feel Sean's arms around me, and it's like he's holding me together.

I'm stalking Mrs. Arnold Mikloshevsky—as if she doesn't have enough problems. I'm sitting outside their house in Mom's purple convertible. I don't know what I'm hoping to see.

Then I see her. She's walking a dog—the yellow Lab I saw last time—and even though I don't know what I was expecting, she's not what I expected, not a frail society-lady or fat or harsh or ugly. Just a middle-aged woman. A mom—anyone's mom but mine. I wonder if she knows her husband doesn't love her anymore.

That's when I start to cry. Sitting there in Mom's stupid, shiny convertible, I cry because my stupid, shiny mother is ruining this woman's life.

I hear a tap on the window. "Are you all right?"

It's the woman. Arnold's . . . Mrs. Arnold. I roll down the window. "I'm fine." I breathe hard through my nose, so I won't sob. "I'm just . . . lost." Which is true, sort of.

"It *is* confusing here. Where are you headed?"

I give her an address—Dad's address, actually, and she starts telling me the directions. The dog stands on its hind legs, putting its front paws on Mom's car's nice, purple finish. Good. "Down, Ginger," she says. "Sorry."

"It's okay," I say. "I always wanted a Lab."

She peers at me. "Do your parents know where you are? I always worried about my girls when they went out at night. Actually, I still worry. You want to call your mother? You can use my phone if you don't have a cell."

I want to say yes. Call my mother. Save yourself. But I don't. It won't matter anyhow. If Arnold's made up his mind, his wife knowing a few weeks earlier won't matter. So I say, "Yes. I mean, I'm okay." I feel a chill and hug myself with both arms. "I'm running an errand for my mom." I tell her the address again, and she gives me the full directions. She even offers to get a sheet of paper to write them down, but I tell her that's not necessary.

I cry the whole way home.

*H*ow's the duet going?" Rowena asks at my voice lesson the following week.

"It's going." I don't add that I am completely getting into the Violetta character by developing a monster crush on Alfredo, a.k.a. Sean.

"You and Sean getting along okay?"

Huge understatement here: "He's fine."

Rowena nods. "I thought you two would make a good pairing."

"Yeah, our voices sound great together."

"Yes, but more than that—Sean seems like a boy who knows what he wants and is willing to work to get it. You're that way too." She takes something from on top of the piano. "That's why I wanted to talk to you. Have you thought about what you're going to do this summer?"

I smile. "Yes, actually. I was thinking about the University of Miami's choral camp." I bet she'll be proud of me for thinking so far ahead. It's only November.

"That's great. But I had another idea that I think is exciting. There's a summer opera program in New York." She shows me the flier in her hand.

"New York?" I say. "Like, the State of New York—miles away? "Start spreading the news . . . That New York?"

"That very New York. Not the city, though. It's farther north. It's opera for high school kids. I have a friend on staff there, and she says if you're as promising as I say you are, you could come stay with her and her family. Of course, you'd have to audition."

"I'd have to fly to New York to audition? Mom would never go for that. She doesn't even like me taking the train to school here."

"All taken care of." Rowena's looking pretty pleased with herself. "You can send a tape. It's due by March—one piece in English, one in a foreign language. You can use the songs we're prepping for competition in February. Think you can handle it?"

"I'm not sure."

"Oh, you have no reason to be nervous. You're the most talented student I've ever had, and that includes college kids. You'll get in for sure."

"That's not it." My mind's racing. I should want to do this. It's all I've ever wanted to do. And yet, part of me just keeps thinking about a gazillion reasons why not. I'd have to try out, and possibly screw up like I did at the auditions for the show at school. And if I did get in, I'd have to go to New York all by myself, when it already took everything I had just to get to Miami High School of the Arts. And then there's Sean. The choral camp is just a one-week thing, but I think I'd go through withdrawal without Sean. I wonder if he could go too. "How long is it?"

"Six weeks. I thought you'd be excited. I know you don't mind getting away."

"Right. It's just . . . no way would my mom let me go for so long."

Liar. Mom's going into Arnold overdrive. She probably wouldn't even notice I was gone, until she got the credit card bill for the plane ticket.

"I'll talk to her." She squints at me. "Is there some other reason. Like a guy?"

"Of course not." *Liar, liar, pants on fire.*

"Caitlin, I remember when I was a teenager." Rowena stops, like she's thinking very hard about what to say next. "I thought the relationships I had were so important—thought they were forever. But they weren't. Very few people end up marrying their high school sweethearts, so it's not worth it to make major decisions—or miss out on important opportunities—for someone who is probably just temporary. And besides, if he's that wonderful, he'd want you to do what's best for you. Being a singer will mean making some sacrifices as far as friends and romance."

"It's not a guy. You know I'm not seeing anyone at school."

Rowena nods. "Yes, I knew there was no one there. I just thought maybe . . . I'm sorry. It was wrong of me to assume."

That's when I realize what she meant, why she's so freaked out.

"I'm not back with Nick," I tell her.

She makes a "sigh of relief" gesture with hand to forehead. "Okay. Then talk to your mom."

I'm not at all sure I will, but I nod.

♪ Opera_Grrrl's Online Journal

Subject: Over the river and thru the woods, 2 Daddy's mansion we go
Date: November 26
Time: 7:18 p.m.
Listening 2: Vienna Boys' Choir Xmas Album
Feeling: Wiped
Weight: 114 lbs. (Holding steady . . . . I barely ate dinner. See below.)

Spent Thxgiving with Daddy-kins. It was actually FUN b/c Courtney (a.k.a. my 1/2 sister, a.k.a. Thing 1) has become a vegetarian so she spent the *entire* time talking about the living conditions of turkeys & how they're overfed 2 fatten their breasts & can barely stand up . . . . and Macy spent the whole time yelling at her and saying she couldn't eat the #@*! turkey she'd spent 5 hrs. cooking. LOL.

I could barely eat either, but that's not a bad thing.

(BTW, did u know that turkey tetrazzini, a fattening use of leftover turkey, was actually named after a diva—Luisa Tetrazzini?)

On the way out, Dad gave me my Xmas gift (a month

early, as usual), a pink iPod mini. "Your mom says u like music," he says.

Très understatement!!!! Can u believe I thought he'd let me live w/ him???? He knows nothing about my life!

After dinner I thought about driving by Arnold's house on the way back 2 see if he's home w/ his family (Mom lent me the car instead of driving me 2 Dad's) but the tryptophan, that stuff in turkey that makes u sleepy, was already kicking in, so I'm here, sacking out.

*T*hanksgiving Friday, in keeping with my theme of avoiding Mom, I try to slip out early. I'm meeting Sean at Rowena's to practice our duet. But Mom stops me.

"Guess what?"

"You're up early." Usually, she can't peel her eyes open until long after I leave.

"Guess I'm excited. You'll never guess what happened."

"I don't have time to guess. I have to go to Rowena's."

"Okay, I'll tell you. Last night, I talked to Arnold on the phone, and I reminded him of how much I wanted to go to the opera . . ."

Note: On the *phone*. So he *does* spend major holidays with his family.

She's still talking. ". . . and he said he was planning on taking me to the very first one . . . La . . . something or other. *La Trap-door.* Anyway, it's two weeks from today."

"That's great, Mom." It's also my opening night—not that I've told her about the performances yet. I also haven't asked her about the summer program in New York. There just hasn't been the right moment yet. There never seems to be a right moment with Mom.

"And there's another thing."

"Mom, I really need to go."

"But it's important." She's practically jumping up and down. "I think he's going to propose. He said he wanted to discuss something really important."

Outside, our neighbor Mrs. Dankes is taking a cereal box out to her garbage can in a pink housecoat and fuzzy slippers. This is what I think about at this point in time, so I won't have to think about the fact that my mother is officially a homewrecker.

"Caitlin?"

"What makes you think he'll propose?"

"I told him I wanted to discuss where our relationship's going. He said he did too, but first he had some things to take care of, so it would have to wait until December. *Then* I asked him about the opera, and he said that was a good idea and we could talk then. He even gave me money and told me to buy something sparkly to wear . . . as if I don't already own something sparkly."

He probably didn't mean a belly button ring.

"He probably meant a gown," I say. "People wear gowns to the opera."

"Yes, a gown." Mom sighs. "I feel like a princess. Caitlin . . . ?"

I'm mulling over the fact that my mother is actually taking

money from a man she's sleeping with, so at first, I don't catch the incredible thing that comes from her mouth.

"Caitlin, you know what to wear to this stuff. Can we go shopping together?"

I stare at her. She's actually asking me for advice?

Rewind. Stop. Play.

Yes. Yes, she's asking me for advice. Sort of.

"Please," she coos. "You always know how to dress . . . less trendy."

Nerdy. Boring. Childish.

"It will be fun, shopping together."

Fun's not the word I'd choose, but I nod. At this point, I'd agree to anything to get myself out of here. "Gotta go now."

"I'm sorry, honey. I didn't ask how it went yesterday with Dad. I'm just so excited."

"Yeah. You said that."

"I know. But please tell me."

"There's nothing to tell. I came, we ate, he gave me an iPod because he heard somewhere that I was into music. It was fine." I look at my watch.

"Are you sure? I always worry that these visits with your father will tear off little pieces of your soul."

"No, it was okay." Actually, what she said sounded really close to the truth, but I have to get out of here before I say something terrible to her. "I'm late."

"All right."

I pick up my sheet music and head for the door.

"Caitlin?"

"What?"

"I know you don't agree, but I really think this will be a good thing for us."

"Mom, I have to go."

She nods, and I shut the door.

W hat are you doing the rest of the day?" I ask Sean after we finish practicing.

It's a gray day. Grayday, grayday, grayday . . . the kind of day when you just feel sad even if you're happy. I should be happy, happy, happy because practicing for our duet went super-well—"It'll be a highlight of the show," Rowena said—and also because Rowena didn't mention anything about the New York summer program in front of Sean. I still haven't decided what to do about that. But instead of being happy, I'm bummed about what Mom told me about Arnold. I don't want to go home—particularly because I don't want to have to go shopping with her on the biggest shopping day of the year.

"Um . . ." Sean fiddles with his car keys. "I'm meeting Rudy at around . . ." He stops. "What's wrong, Caitlin?"

And that's all it takes for me to pour out the whole pathetic Mom/Arnold story. Even while I'm doing it, I'm thinking, *What are you, stupid?* I'd never have told any of my old friends something this personal and embarrassing. On top of the Nick thing too. But I've known Sean and Gigi a couple of months, and they already know all the gory details.

When I finish, Sean says all the appropriate, *It'll be okays,* then adds, "Know what I'm in the mood for?"

"A break from me and my problems?" But I'm hoping he'll say, *I'm in the mood to kiss you* or *I want to scrape the dust of this sorry town off my shoes and fly with you to Paris.* Not likely.

He laughs. "A Slurpee. Is there a Seven-Eleven near you?"

We drive to a 7-Eleven near the beach. They have a machine with eight Slurpee flavors, but two spigots are broken. Sean says we should both get a large and both get three flavors, so we can try them all. So I get white cherry, Coke, and blueberry, while Sean gets what he calls a "tropical blend" of lime, banana, and Spongebob piña colada. "You should work for Seven-Eleven," I say. "In the flavor development."

"Right. And after I design the perfect flavor, they'll pay me a lot of money and finance my opera career." He holds out his cup to me. "Want some?"

I take a sip, wondering if sharing his straw is the closest I'll ever get to kissing him. Pretty gross, right, wanting to suck some-one's spit off a straw . . . Most girls I know would rather sleep with a guy. "Try mine too," I say.

"You kids plan on paying for those?" the counter guy asks.

We do, and we decide to cross the street and drink them on the beach. "Should we drive?" I ask. "The weather looks pretty bad." The clouds are hanging low, making different shades of black against the sky, so it looks like steps to heaven.

"Nah, let's walk. It'll be okay."

So we do, skipping across the six-lane highway toward the roaring ocean. The clouds seem dark and the breeze is cool, cooler still with the Slurpee. I shiver.

"You're cold?" Sean asks.

"I don't want to go home." *BIG understatement.* My teeth chatter. "I'm f—fine."

"Here." He unbuttons the long-sleeved shirt he has on over his T-shirt and hands it to me. It's old, soft, and smells like Sean, and as our feet crunch the sand, I hold the collar to my nose and know that, forever and ever, when I smell that smell, or even smell the ocean, or a piña colada Slurpee, I will think of him.

"But take your shoes off," he says. "No point walking on the beach with shoes."

I sit and remove them, obedient, and leave them by the roadside. I let my toes sink deep into the cold sand. Sean takes his off too. He stands and holds his hand out to me. I reach for his fingers, thinking, *Kiss me. Kiss me.*

He doesn't. I take a sip of my Slurpee, a small one because I don't want it to end.

"Know where I was Thanksgiving Friday last year?" I say.

"Where? Some football game with your cool cheergirl friends?" He mimes lame-looking pom-pom moves.

I make a face. "Close. In Key West with them. We went snorkeling one day. I remember one of the guys saw a shark under the reef." I'd almost forgotten about this. It seems so long ago.

"Cool. Did you see it?"

I nod. "It was just this little lemon shark, but I was freaking out. I was petrified. And Nick, my boyfriend, he was telling me don't worry about it, I didn't have to dive down if I didn't want to, but . . ." I stop. It's hard to explain so Sean will understand, and I don't even really know why I'm telling him this. "But I *wanted* to see the shark, even though I was scared. I didn't want to let being afraid make me miss out on something. I wanted to face it and know that I would be okay. You know? So I dove down and saw it."

"Yeah?" Sean offers me his Slurpee. "I like that story."

"Yeah, I do too." I take a sip of his Slurpee and give him mine. "It makes me sound sort of brave."

"You *are* brave."

I feel a drop of water on my face. I don't say anything, hoping maybe it's just a spray from the ocean. But I feel another drop— a fat one—then another.

"And . . . you were right," Sean says. "We should head back."

"Guess so." I turn real slow, as four more drops splash my face and shoulders.

"We'd better run," he says. "Sorry."

We begin to run. The drops are harder now, too many to count. I feel them soaking through Sean's shirt, making it cling to me. It's hard to run in the sand—harder still in the rain—and we're really far from Sean's car. I stumble and drop the Slurpee. It falls to the sand, and I fall after it. "Sorry. You go ahead! I'm sorry."

"Right. I'll just leave you here." He holds out his hand. The rain is getting into my eyes, my mouth. He pulls me up. I'm drowning, and Sean's hand is pulling me to safety. "I don't think we can get any wetter," he says. "Let's just walk."

We stumble along, holding each other, giggling.

"I'm sorry," he says again when we reach the car. "I'll remember from now on—take Caitlin's advice on weather issues."

"I don't mind. It was an adventure."

"I was hoping you'd see it that way, instead of seeing it as stupid Sean making you get all soaked just to drink Slurpees on the beach."

He turns on the car's heater to dry us off. My shoes are still back on the sand, but I don't bring it up. Instead, I move closer to the heat and to him. We're so close, and I can feel how it was with his hand on me. Again, I think he should kiss me.

He says. "Great practice today, huh?"

"Yeah." The rain is coming down outside, but the heat inside is warm and nice. I lean closer.

He sits straight instead, and aims the vent toward me. "Want some more of my Slurpee?"

"What?"

"Do you want some of my Slurpee—since you dropped yours?"

And suddenly it all comes together, and I get it: He's never going to kiss me.

I pull off the now-soaked shirt he lent me and look out the window, letting that piece of knowledge sink in like a thousand raindrops. I don't say anything. Sean doesn't either, and I'm glad. It's like a head-slap moment. I've figured out what was right in front of me the whole time. Duh.

I shake my head. "So you're going out with Rudy today?"

"What?"

I'm still not looking at him—I can't—but he sounds surprised, like he forgot I was there. "Oh, yeah. It's his sister's birthday. It'll be me, Rudy, and a cast of thousands of his cousins." He laughs. "I think they're roasting a pig in the yard."

"How long have you and Rudy . . ." I make myself look at him and finish the sentence. ". . . been together?"

He smiles. "Choral Camp last summer. We met the first day and it was . . . You ever meet someone and just click with them? Like, everything about them is interesting, and you know it's the same way for them with you?"

"Not yet," I say. *Except with you.* Outside the car, the rain's still pounding, drowning us, and I feel so completely stupid I can barely speak.

"Well, someday you will, I bet. You'll meet someone who even likes opera." He grins again. "I wasn't sure if you knew about Rudy and me."

I have to say something. "Oh, sure. It's completely . . . obvious you two are a . . . couple."

He nods. "Well, at my old school, it wouldn't have been

completely obvious. It's still pretty . . . weird there. Most people there thought Misty and me were together, since we were such good friends. And when I got here, I figured people in the arts are more, you know, accepting, but I still thought I don't have to give people info they don't need."

I nod. It's still hard to talk and look at him too. I mean, yeah, I figured it out, but I was still hoping I was wrong. So I put my arms around his neck and hug him hard and manage to get out, "I know."

And I do.

But for some reason, I still feel exactly like that day with the shark.

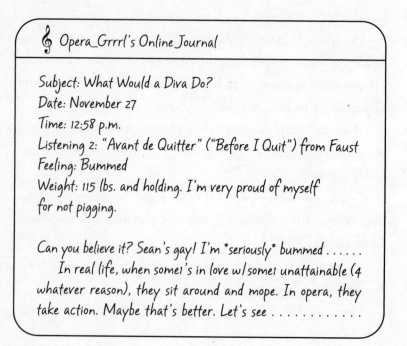

♪ Opera_Grrrl's Online Journal

Subject: What Would a Diva Do?
Date: November 27
Time: 12:58 p.m.
Listening 2: "Avant de Quitter" ("Before I Quit") from Faust
Feeling: Bummed
Weight: 115 lbs. and holding. I'm very proud of myself for not pigging.

Can you believe it? Sean's gay! I'm *seriously* bummed . . . . . .
     In real life, when some1's in love w/ some1 unattainable (4 whatever reason), they sit around and mope. In opera, they take action. Maybe that's better. Let's see . . . .

What do people in operas do???

MADAME BUTTERFLY–Commit ritual suicide (but I don't know any rituals).
RIGOLETTO–Step in the path of a hired assassin (don't know any of those either).
PAGLIACCI–Murder (trying 2 find a solution that avoids jail and/or death).
CARMEN–Ditto
IL TABARRO–Ditto (Seeing a pattern here?).
CAVALLERIA RUSTICANA–Get some1 else mad enough at the guy that *they* commit the murder.
In UN BALLO IN MASCHERA, Amelia goes 2 the grave-yard & picks some special plants 2 make her forget the guy . . . . but then he sees her & they make out . . . . . . all of which leads 2 . . . . MURDER.

It seems like an awful lot of operas end with murderers singing sorrowfully over the bodies of their beloved victims. I don't want 2 kill Sean. He's my best friend, and I love him.

Okay, so I'll mope.

*O*n Sunday, Sean makes his long-promised visit to come help me with my dance steps. Now that the possibility of romance is zip, zilch, zero, nothing, nada, I would have thought I wouldn't be as excited about having Sean over. But it's really weird because I am excited. Maybe it has something to do with the fact that our performance is in two weeks and there's still the constant threat of having to sing on the side of the stage like a defective. Or maybe I just love being with Sean that much, even if I can't *love*-love him.

Mom has an open house that actually (yessss!) does happen. We practice our duet, then go over dance steps about fifteen times. We even get out the camera that Mom uses to make "digital tours" of the homes she's listed. I film Sean dancing. "I promise to watch it every day."

"You'd better," he says. "You can do it."

"I will, I will." I actually think I can.

Then, since it's still an hour before Mom gets home, we order a pizza, and film each other singing. We're making up an opera about school. I play Ms. Wolfe, and Sean does a hilarious Miss Lorraine Davis, staggering on tiptoe, singing, "Art is suffering, my children! Suffer for art!" in a falsetto voice.

Later, while we're eating pizza, Sean says, "Caitlin, you may be the perfect girl."

A week ago, when I was thinking of Sean as the possible Man of My Dreams, this would have caused my stomach to lurch like I'm on the Tower of Terror ride at Disney, where you don't know if you're up or down. I may have actually been unable to speak. Now I smile and say, "Why?" *Like a normal person.*

"Well, you're not only beautiful and talented. You are also the only girl on the planet—maybe the only human being—who likes pepperoni and olive pizza like I do."

I laugh. "You're right. Usually, if people like pepperoni, they aren't into olives, and if they like olives, they want a veggie and think the pepperoni is too fatty."

"Not us, huh? We're naturally skinny."

I stare at him like, *Are you blind, boy?* "Not me. I was fat for years."

"Really?"

"I was hideous."

"I doubt that."

I reach across him to the end table where Mom keeps our old photos. A week ago, I wouldn't have done this either, but I find my freshman class picture. "See?"

He takes it. I expect him to recoil in horror. *No! No! This swamp thing can't possibly be you!* Instead, he grins. "You look so cute with pigtails."

I stare at him. "Right."

"Yeah." He looks at the photo again. "I mean, maybe you're not a model type like now. What do you weigh, a hundred pounds? But you were so cute. Look."

He shows me the photo. I stare at it, at me, trying to look like Lizzie McGuire in braids, grinning like crazy. It's like I've never seen the photo before, or that person. Sean's right. I *was* cute. I weighed over twenty pounds more than now—thirty-five pounds more than my thinnest—which is not *that* big. I wasn't a beast. I was cute. I say, "You really think I look like a model?"

He nods and hands back the photo. "You're beautiful."

That's when the door flies open and my mother does a happy dance across the living room. "Someone made a full-price offer, Caitlin! We get to eat this month!"

Which is, of course, an exaggeration. We eat every month. Dad pays.

She sees Sean. "Oh, you have company." She walks closer. "And pizza . . . oh, but you got pepperoni. I'll have to pick that off. Too fatty."

I see Sean stifle a laugh, then wink at me. Of course, that's exactly what we said everyone does. I wink back, and it feels good to be with him, good and warm and comfortable.

196

"What?" Mom says. "What?"

"Nothing, Mom. Get a plate. There's a slice here with hardly any pepperoni. We should've gotten a veggie."

As soon as she walks out, Sean and I burst into silent giggles.

owena corners me on the way out of her class Tuesday. "Did you talk to your mother?"

I know what she means. *Did I talk to my mother about the summer opera program?* The answer is no. No, I didn't.

"Yeah. Yeah, I did. She said no."

I don't know why I didn't ask, except that I just wasn't sure I wanted to go. I want to just enjoy where I am for a while, and not have to leave. Still, I'm surprised when Rowena says, "Caitlin, are you sure you asked her?"

"What? Of course I did. What would make you say something like that?"

"Caitlin, I know that to some people, the idea of success can be as scary as failure."

"What does that mean? That makes no sense."

"I think it does. If you fail, that's comfortable. Nothing changes, right? You can stay exactly where you are."

"I don't want to do that. That's why I transferred schools.

I wanted a change."

"I know when your acceptance letter went out. I know you thought long and hard about whether to transfer. I doubt you would have if it hadn't been for my pressure."

I look away. "That was because my mother—"

"Your parents don't support your dreams. Which makes it easy to sit back and say that you can't do it. But there are people who have overcome worse adversity to make their dreams come true. It isn't always easy or comfortable."

I think of Sean again and what he said about tenacity. Am I *un*-tenacious because I don't want to pick up and leave everything again—because I don't want to go someplace where I might not be that talented? "I don't expect it to be easy."

"I hope not, because it won't be. But that doesn't mean you can't do it. It just means you have to want it. And you have to want it more than anything else."

"I do want it. Really, my mother said no. I'm sorry you don't believe me."

Rowena relents. "Okay, I'm sorry. Do you think it would help if I talked to her?"

"No!" I look over at Gigi, who's waiting for me near the door. "I mean, no, I don't think so." I'm lying like the proverbial rug now. "My mom . . . we've been having some problems. Money stuff. She says I need to get a job over the summer."

"Oh, I see." Rowena looks surprised. Finances aren't usually a problem in our neighborhood.

I say, "But if there's something near here, I could go during the day and work nights."

"Okay." Rowena pats my hand. "We'll find something wonderful for you to do this summer. Don't worry."

I head for the door, not looking at Rowena.

"What'd she want?" Gigi asks, when I get into the hall.

"Oh, nothing. There's just a lesson I need to reschedule."

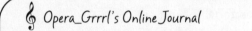 Opera_Grrrl's Online Journal

Subject: Lies
Date: December 1
Time: 8:14 p.m.
Feeling: Confused
Weight: 115 lbs.

I lied 2 Rowena . . . . Mom might have said no, but she might have said yes 2, since she just sold a house (an expensive 1 around here) and has some $$, and also b/c it would give her more time 2 play kissy-face w/ Arnold . . . . & now, of course, there's not the whole issue of a relationship with Sean. But . . . . I don't know. The idea of sending a tape & then waiting 2 see if I get rejected just sort of makes me feel sick . . . . not 2 mention having 2 go someplace new 4 the whole summer. New place, new people. It was hard enough coming here, and now I just sort of got used 2 it & am happy w/ where I am.

Rowena thinks I'm afraid 2 try 2 be successful. That's just crazy. Who fears success???? I want 2 be successful. Why wouldn't I??? I just want 2 be successful here . . . . for a while.

Shopping with Mom during Christmas season. "Joy to the World" doesn't begin to cover it. My plan, basically, is to make sure she's dressed completely wrong for the opera, that is to say, let her buy the type of thing she usually wants—the three Bs: Bare midriff, Bustier, and Butt cleavage. It's the least I can do for Arnold's soon-to-be-ex-wife and soon-to-be-ex-dog.

Arnold actually gave Mom a *thousand* dollars to buy a dress, and the whole way to the Falls, Mom sits in the driver's seat of ye olde purple convertible, talking about Arnold in fishing terms—hook, line, and sinker; reel him in; cast the net. But when we pull into our parking space, Mom clutches my arm.

"I am soooo glad you came with me."

"What?"

"It's just . . . I wouldn't know how to dress around opera people!"

I stare at her. And then I feel the steel bars of my resolve melting. Melting, I tell you. I can't send her out there looking stupid, if she *knows* she looks stupid. I can't.

"It's fine," I say. "Come on. Let's get down to some serious shopping."

Play the shopping montage scene here (like the one in *Pretty Woman,* where Richard Gere took the hooker to Rodeo Drive). Mom and me at Macy's, trying on satin, taffeta, and velvet; in Bloomingdales, putting makeup samples on each other; and at Mayors, trying on real jewelry we *definitely* aren't buying. Since it's nearly Christmas, I choose a black velvet dress with a dark green satin sash and a bare back—but no butt cleavage. Then we go downstairs to choose shoes.

"How about these?" Mom holds up a pair of silver high-heeled sandals.

"Too sexy," I tell her. It's fun playing *What Not to Wear,* saying what I actually *think* for once.

We finally get her into some black satin slingbacks with an open side and what Mom calls "toe cleavage" (the only cleavage I'd let her show) and some real-looking fake diamond and emerald earrings. We're almost finished with our shopping trip and, so far, we've done a decent job of avoiding taboo topics, such as her dating a married man.

On the way out, we pass Jessica McClintock. Mom looks in the window.

"Uh-uh, Mom. Waaaay too young. That's where my friends shop for prom dresses. You want to look sophisticated." *This is fun.*

She puts her hand on my elbow. "I know, I know. I didn't mean for me."

She guides me into the shop and points to the most beautiful teal blue satin, full-skirted dress. "Do you have a dance or something coming up?"

The dress would be perfect for my opera scene. I was going to wear my last year's Homecoming dress, but this is even better. "We can't afford it."

"I didn't spend all the money Arnold gave me," she says, showing me three hundred-dollar bills.

That's just about what a plane ticket to New York would cost. I could ask her about the summer program. But she says, "Just try it on." And I do. It won't fit me anyway—it's a size three. So I let her lead me into the fitting room.

"Remember that time when I was thirteen and I got stuck inside the dress I was wearing to Derek Wayne's bar mitzvah?" I ask her.

Mom giggles. "That was pretty funny."

"It was not. I had to be cut out of it. It was totally humiliating." I can still picture it: me, lying on my bed, squealing like a pig, while Mom took her pruning shears to the pink satin.

"Here, let me get that." Mom turns me around so my back is toward her, then zips the dress in one move. "No problems now. You look perfect."

I stare at my reflection. The dress fits great, and I look like a professional opera singer in it. I could be playing Juliet, singing her waltz song, or Marguerite in *Faust*, before she gets pregnant and arrested and dies, or Violetta, or . . . "Can I have it?"

Mom nods.

At the cash register, she's still bubbling. "You look great. We'll look like sisters."

I roll my eyes, but turn away so she can't see me doing it. When I don't answer, she says, "You know what I wish?"

"What?"

"I wish you would like me, Caitlin. You used to."

I'd been thinking the same thing, but I say, "Of course I like you."

She gives me this look like, *Yeah, right*, and says, "Well, I guess we should pay for the dress before we find something else."

♪ Opera_Grrrl's Online Journal

Subject: Shopping (Guilt) Trip
Date: December 2
Time: 4:35 p.m.
Listening 2: "Martern Aller Arten" ("Tortures Unabating")
from *The Abduction from the Seraglio*
Feeling: Tired
Weight: 116 lbs.

Shopping w/ Mom 2day. It reminded me of when I was little and yet, fat, and Mom was this life-sized Barbie doll. We'd go shopping & I could live vicariously thru her—trying short skirts on her skinny body and satin bustiers on her perfect breasts. Back then, I was sooo proud that my mom was prettier than every1 else's. She'd tell me that once I lost that "baby fat" I'd be beautiful— and then we'd go buy Häagen-Dazs at the food court. Once upon a time, I wanted 2 be just like her.

2day, I pretended I still do . . . . When I used 2 like Mom, it was comfortable, like nothing could ever hurt me. I wish I could tell her everything, about Sean and how stupid I was not 2 figure out about him and Rudy sooner, about how right she was about Dad, and about how scared I am of not being good enough, or maybe being good enough . . . . . . I haven't talked 2 her in so long, since I grew up and learned what was what. I wonder if I could again.

But I remember Mrs. Arnold and . . . . I can't.

I was thinking about what you said before," I say.

Mom's sitting on the sofa in the living room. She has her shoes off and her toes are in those foamy things that separate them to keep the polish from getting messed up. Now, she's painting her fingernails a blood red. It's Saturday night, and she has no date.

"Oh, Caitlin, come sit with me." She points at her toenails. "It's a 'repairing night.' Want me to do your toes? I was going to start a movie, but my nails are wet. Remember when we used to watch *Pretty Woman* together? It would be so fun."

I shake my head. "I'm going out. But I can put the DVD in for you."

"Thanks." She gestures toward it.

I go pick it up, then stop. "After we talk." I handled the whole Sean thing, and that's made me brave, maybe? Maybe it's time to stop avoiding Mom.

She fans her nails back and forth, looking at me but not *really* looking at me. "Sure. What did you want to talk about?"

"About Arnold."

She fans faster. "Oh, Caitlin, we've been over this."

"I know. But this afternoon, you said something. You said you wished I liked you, like I used to when I was little . . . younger."

"Oh, I'm sorry. I shouldn't have said that. I was just being silly. We had a great time today, and I screwed it up."

"No, you were right. When I was little, I used to look up to you. You were a role model."

"I suppose all mothers and daughters drift apart. When I was a teenager, I thought my mother was just a drone who did the laundry." She stops fanning her nails and tests one, holding it to her lip. "It's dry. Can you hand me that DVD?"

"Mom, I want to talk."

"Caitlin, there's nothing to talk about here."

"But you're dating a married man. It's wrong."

"It's not much of a marriage anymore. He told me they haven't been in love for a long time."

"But how do you know? And how do you know he won't do the same thing to you, if he could do it to her?" Trying to appeal to her selfish side—a big side.

"Caitlin, it's complicated."

"I went to see her."

"Who?"

"Arnold's wife. I talked to her."

She stands and makes an *I'm so shocked* gesture, knocking her freshly polished hand into the lamp. She looks at it and curses. It wasn't dry. "You *talked* to her?"

"Yes." I'm sort of enjoying that she's freaking out. Actually, really enjoying it.

"When? What did you say?" She looks from her nail to the phone, like she's thinking about calling Arnold to do some kind of damage control. "Oh, Caitlin, what did you do?"

"She's a nice lady, Mom," I say, still not giving her the information she wants. I actually *love* that she's in total freak-out mode. Maybe it will bring her to her senses. "They have a yellow Lab. Did you know that? And she told me about how she worries about her daughters when they're out at night."

"Caitlin, when was this? When did you talk to her?" She's fanning her hands so much it looks like she might take off. "How could you do this to me?"

"How can you do this to *her*, Mom? You got dumped by Dad. You know what it's like. How can you put someone else through that? How can you be like this?"

"Caitlin? Answer my question."

"Answer mine!"

She reaches for the phone. "I have to call him."

"So you don't care what I think? You only care about him." When she doesn't answer, I say, "Look, I didn't tell her about you and Arnold. I . . . couldn't. But I wanted to. I wanted her to know because it isn't fair."

"Fair?" She plunks down the phone. "Fair? Is it fair that I'm here all by myself while your father has everything? Is it fair that you'll go to college soon, and I'll be old and fat and alone?"

"You'll never be fat," I say. "You're thin and perfect, and you don't even diet. You're never lonely either."

"You don't know anything about me. And you're the one that got me thinking this way."

"What way?"

"About the future. That I need to get married, to find some-one who can sup— be with me. When you said what you said last summer, I realized I could end up with nothing."

"What did I say?"

"What you said last summer. You could leave, and I'd have no one, nothing. I'd be all alone." She looks away. "That's when I knew I needed someone like Arnold."

Oh, God. When I'd threatened to leave and take Dad's child support with me, that was a wake-up call. She realized her free ride might be over. It will be over when I hit eighteen anyway. And that makes me so mad, thinking that all these years, I'd been noth-ing but a meal ticket to her, and now Arnold is her meal ticket, and she doesn't care who she hurts.

I say it. The instant after I think all those things, I say them. All of them. And then I keep going. I scream, "I can't believe you. You're that lazy? Maybe if you stopped worrying for two seconds about your bikini wax and your nails . . ." I knock against her hand. ". . . And getting a man, you could get a real job and not have to leech off Dad!"

I stop yelling, but I can still hear the words. My ears feel tight with them. I can almost see them, as if they exist in some physical form.

She stands there a moment, and then she lunges for me, like she's going to hit me. In my whole life, she's never hit me, and she doesn't this time either. Instead, she starts screaming, "You little brat! You think you know everything! You think you're better than me? You have the world at your feet, and it's because of me! Me! You think that scumbag father of yours would do one thing he's not court-ordered to?"

She keeps on like that, screaming ugly things about Dad, things I can't even argue with. I know they're true. And I just stand there, staring, trying not to blink because if I blink, I'll cry. And I won't give her the satisfaction.

She keeps going. "I could have been something, but instead, I had you. You think I wanted to be thirty-seven with a daughter who thinks she's so hot? I used to be hot too. You are exactly like I was!"

Well, this is too much. Better to be slapped physically. Worse to be compared to her. I feel the first tear starting down my cheek, but before she can see it, I scream, "I am nothing like you!"

And I run.

Subject: Tortures and Triumphs
Date: December 3
Time: 11:11 p.m.
Listening 2: "Triumphal March" from Aïda
Feeling: Triumphant
Weight: 114 lbs. (purely by accident, haven't been dieting @ all)

You'd think when I mastered the dance steps after tremendous personal sacrifice that Ms. Wolfe might—just might—have something 2 say. Something like, "Good job, Caitlin" or "Hard work really paid off."

Nah. I didn't think so either.

2day @ rehearsal, I failed 2 screw up for the 1st time, and Ms. Wolfe failed 2 yell at me . . . . for the 1st time.

But when we finished our approximately 900th run-thru of the dance numbers, she faced us w/ her usual doglike expression.

She pointed @ a redheaded girl who was previously the 2nd worst dancer. "Ainsley! There are a few 2 many dancers. Just sing on the side of the stage."

I struggled w/2 impulses: wanting 2 give Ainsley some kind of sympathetic look and not wanting 2 draw attention 2 myself. I didn't move. Next, Ms. Wolfe singled out 2 fatgirls who danced OK but the 90-lb. Ms. Wolfe probably thought they wouldn't look great in the costume (leotards w/ glittery vests over them) and told them the same thing. That bugged me. I noticed she didn't pull any guys out, even tho there were several who were worse than the girls that she cut. Guys are held 2 a completely different standard here, or, as Gigi says, "If you have a penis, you don't *need* talent." Speaking of which, Gus still has no jockstrap, and when he's in the room, it's hard 2 look @ anything else . . . . though we all try.

Finally, Ms. Wolfe got to me. She gave me a long look, & I thought for sure she'd cut me. I knew if that happened, after all my work, I'd burst into tears or just plain burst. What if she didn't notice my failure 2 screw up 2day & just remembered the 8,000 times I was bad???

But finally, she clapped her hands and told us 2 do it 1 more time.

And I breathed. Sean reached over 2 hi-5 me, & Gigi grinned, but I shook my head. I didn't want 2 jinx it.

But on the inside, I felt like I could do grandes jetés if I wanted!

On Friday, I go early to Rowena's office. I feel tremendously guilty over the New York thing, so I want to smooth things over with her. I want to do what she tells me, but I don't want to. When I get there, I have to wait because she has a student in there, a blond girl. I recognize her as one of the students who sang at the *La Traviata* auditions, one of the less-good ones.

They're in there a really long time, but just as I decide to give up, she runs out. She's crying, and Rowena comes to the door, too, yelling, "Mary! Wait!" But the girl doesn't stop. That's when Rowena notices me there.

"This is a bad time?" I ask.

Rowena sighs. "No . . . I mean, it's always hard."

"What is?"

"Having to tell a student she should change majors—that I don't think she'll make it in performance and she should consider music education or merchandising instead."

"That's what you told her?" I'm thinking, *I'd die.*

Rowena nods. "She was promising at auditions last year, but she hasn't improved much. I understand she parties quite a bit, and it doesn't seem like the commitment's there. You have to want it more than anything. You have to sacrifice."

Sacrifice. I think about the New York program. "What will happen to her now?"

"She has to decide. She can change majors, which is what I suggested. Or she can decide I don't know what I'm talking about. Maybe she'll take it as a challenge and practice more and show me I'm wrong. It's her choice."

"Am I good enough?" I say.

"Caitlin, this isn't about you."

"But it could be. You said she seemed promising last year at auditions. You never can tell, right?"

"I can tell. I know you. And I know you're very committed."

"Am I?" I feel my headache right down in my neck. If I had to sing now, I couldn't. I want to confess my lie about New York. But Mom's so furious with me now, she probably *would* say no if I asked her.

"Yes. You're one of my most talented students ever." She touches my hand. "Don't worry. Just keep doing what you're doing."

At lunch, I tell Gigi about it—not about lying to Rowena because I know what she'd say (she'd kill me!), but about Mary.

Gigi rolls her eyes. "You said yourself the girl wasn't very good. Rowena probably did her a huge favor. Why does it bother you?"

"But can you imagine not singing anymore? Why wake up in the morning?"

"But that's how *you* feel about it. If she felt that way, she'd have practiced more. Then she wouldn't be getting this news."

"I guess."

"Absolutely. It's like a reality show where they vote the weaklings off first. When you're five and dancing in your mom's dresses, everyone's a superstar. But then some people get picked to be 'listeners' in music class, and others don't make the good chorus in middle school, and others don't get in here. And some people screw up. But that's not you, Cait. You can make it."

"I guess," I repeat.

But that night and both days of the weekend, I sing scales for an extra hour.

*F*or the next week, I own you." Miss Davis teeters for a second, allowing this shocking news to sink in. It's the Monday before the show. "Homework in your academic classes? Unimportant. Family and friends don't exist. Exercise? Burn calories onstage. Your love life?" She takes a long look at Gus and Misty, who are attempting to merge into one person. "Not on my time. And make no mistake about it—your every waking moment is my time. I'm not about balance." She stares at us. "Understand?"

We all nod, somberly, like we're supposed to. Even Gigi.

"Good. Places for the opening number." We start to file offstage. Miss Davis holds out a painted claw, and fixes on Gus. "You!"

Gus executes a comic stop and gestures like, *Me?*

"Yes, you. Purchase an athletic supporter."

"Why?"

"Because your . . . equipment is showing. If you don't find one by tomorrow, I'll take you shopping during lunch."

We're all trying real hard not to laugh, but someone (I'm not sure it wasn't me) lets out a high-pitched giggle, and then we're all cracking up.

Through it, I hear Gus. "Miss Davis?"

A sigh. "Yes, Gus?"

"If I'm not s'posed to be doing anything but practicing, when do I shop?"

I don't even hear Miss Davis's answer. But the rest of the afternoon, every time I pass Sean or Gigi, we say things like, "Excuse me? Do you happen to have your equipment with you?" or "Can you get your equipment? I need to change a lightbulb."

Sean drives me home after rehearsal.

"How's it going?" he says.

"Great. We'll be rehearsing so much I'll hardly see my mother."

He laughs. "Yeah, all I can think about is this show. Would you believe the other day, I woke up, and my hand was stiff? I'd been doing jazz hands in my sleep!"

"What I can't believe is that three months ago, I'd never *heard* of a jazz hand. And now . . ." I make a gesture like my hand is stuck that way, fingers straight and stiff.

"You're really improving at dance."

"Thanks to you."

"No. Thanks to you." He pulls into my driveway and stops the car. The lights are off inside the house, but I can see Harold the flamingo, who's now dressed like Santa Claus. Sean pulls me toward him and hugs me, and it's different than other times, because I know it's just a hug; a friend-hug and nothing more.

When we part, I say, "So, do you think Gus went and found an all-night sporting-goods store Monday night?"

Sean laughs. "I bet he did. I wouldn't want to go shopping for a jockstrap with Miss Davis!"

♪ Opera_Grrrl's Online Journal

Subject: Sean
Date: December 7
Time: 11:35p.m.
Listening 2: "Che Gelida Manina" from La Bohème
(w/ headphones so as not 2 incur the wrath of Mom)
Feeling: Tired
Weight: 112 lbs. (I think I lost weight from dancing so much)

I've spent a LOT of time thinking about the whole Sean thing, and what I've figured out is: everything happens for a reason . . . . All my life, I wanted 2 be thin & have a boyfriend, but when I did finally get a boyfriend, it didn't work out w/ him . . . . in fact, he HURT ME . . . . and it didn't work out w/ the next guy either . . . . & what I figured out is that I DON'T WANT A BOYFRIEND at this particular moment of my life. I think maybe what I need is a friend & w/ Sean, I have that. I have that more than I've ever had that in my life. And what's more, he's SAFE. I can love him, and he isn't going 2 hurt me, isn't going 2 try and make me be some1 else. Does that make sense????????? I don't even know if it does, & maybe any1 reading this will think I'm crazy (I don't even know if any1 does read this) but I think it's right. And what's more, I think it's more important 2 be w/ some1 b/c you actually care about that person, than being w/ some1 2 be w/ someone.

I don't know what I mean 2 say. But I know what I THINK: I'm happy.

Six-thirty Thursday. We're assembled in our costumes for dress rehearsal. The opening number is a medley of what Miss Davis calls rah-rah, let's-put-on-a-show tunes—"There's No Business Like Show Business," "Applause," "The Lullaby of Broadway," etc. I'm dressed as a stagehand in overalls and a T-shirt, wearing a ton of Mom's Emma Leigh samples. In fact, Mom doesn't know it, but she donated makeup for most of the cast. I still haven't told her about the performance this weekend and I don't know if I will. I'm still that mad at her.

I stand near Gigi. Actually, *behind* Gigi. The good dancers are in front, while the "good singers" like me bring up the rear. At least I'm not on the side of the stage! I look around at the shadows behind me. My friends. I've only known them a few months, but we've bonded together working on this show. The lights fade, and I stare out at where the audience will be tomorrow. The music starts, and I feel a ripple down my spine as the follow spot hits Sylvanie, and she sings her first line:

"Welcome to the theater, to the magic, to the fun . . ."

It's the same line Miss Davis quoted that first day. I didn't know what it was from then, but now, I know it's from a show called *Applause*. Applause. I love applause. That's why I came here. I wanted—and still want—to be in the show.

The rest of the dress rehearsal goes pretty much as it should. I forget my steps twice, but I smile big like Ms. Wolfe told us, and go on like nothing happened. It's too late for her to make me a side-singer. When it comes time for my duet with Sean, I get there early and wait in the wings in my satin dress (trying not to think about the fact that Arnold paid for it), the two drama students do the lead-in for our song. Halfway through, Sean joins me. I feel his hand on my arm.

"The script's pretty lame," I whisper.

"Yeah, but *you* class it up."

The two girls finish their scene, and I have to bite my lip to keep from grinning as we go out to do Violetta's death scene.

Sean is the perfect Alfredo, and I die beautifully.

The only numbers after ours are the classic Broadway scenes and the finale. Gigi's in the classic Broadway section, doing "If My Friends Could See Me Now," a song-and-dance number from *Sweet Charity*. At this point, I've seen her do it approximately seven hundred times, so I head backstage to change into leotard and tights, vest and top hat, for the finale. I walk to the mirror to check how I look. I suck in my stomach. Someone steps beside me.

It's Rowena. "Hey." She squeezes my shoulder. "I just came back to tell you, all the faculty are raving about your performance."

"Thanks." I smile.

"I was thinking about that summer program," Rowena continues. "I'm so sorry you're not going."

"Me too." I reach down to fiddle with the strap of my character shoe.

"I was thinking that maybe if *I* had a word with your mother, it could help her understand what a great opportunity this is. Maybe you could get a part-time job in New York."

"Oh, I don't think so." I unbuckle my shoe entirely, to keep from having to look at Rowena. From the monitor in the dressing room, I hear Gigi's song start. Only two more numbers left until I'm onstage. Can I make this strap last two more songs? "My mom's not even coming to the show."

"Not coming? Are you sure?"

"Absolutely. She doesn't want to come. She hates my being in performing arts." It's not a total lie. Mom isn't coming. She could have asked when the show is, but she's too worried about her own stuff to bother. Tomorrow's the night she goes out on her big date with Arnold—possibly making him my stepfather-to-be.

I need to change the subject. "Is this what it was like, being an opera singer? Did you always feel so excited when you went onstage?"

Rowena nods. I know she's going to say something else about

Mom. So I ask another question.

"Do you ever miss it?"

She shrugs and smiles. "Sure I do. You can't do something every day of your life, dream about it every night, without missing it when it's gone. But I had a great time singing, and now I've moved on to teaching, which I love just as much. Being a singer meant sacrifices as far as family, friends, a normal life go." She looks me in the eye. "On the other hand, if I hadn't taken my shot at it, I might have had a lot of regrets."

I know what she means. I try to think of something to say. But at that moment, there's a scream from the television monitor. The music stops.

Gigi!

I leave my shoe unbuckled and stand. My head feels full and black, like I might faint from rising too quickly. I grab Rowena for support, but she's already headed to the monitor herself. I grab a chair and, once I feel steadier, I push across the room. People are crushed against the monitor. I hear the words, "fell" and "still there." I know that if Gigi could, she'd get up and finish her dance number. If the music stopped, she must be hurt. Rowena's ahead of me, pushing through the crowd toward the stage. I grab her hand and follow.

When I get there, Gigi's on the floor. Ms. Wolfe is next to her, holding her hand. She sees Rowena and yells, "Call a doctor!"

"I can stay with her," I say.

Ms. Wolfe nods and heads backstage. Miss Davis is already

there, yelling, "Be calm, children!"

"I'm fine," Gigi moans. "The show must go on, right?" She starts to stand, grimaces, then sinks back onto the floor, holding her knee.

"Does it hurt a lot?" I say.

"No, I'm just on the floor for no reason!" she snaps.

"Sorry."

"No, I'm sorry." She squeezes my hand hard. "I'm getting up now." She winces. "Okay, maybe just another minute."

"Just stay still. They're calling a doctor to see if they should move you."

She lets fly a choice list of obscenities. "My mom's going to freak. She always thinks something's going to happen to me. 'You're all I have,' she says."

I can't believe it. Just like my mom. "You want me to call and tell her you fell but you're okay?"

She nods and squeezes my hand again. "Cait, what if I tore something? What if I can't be in the show? What if I can't dance anymore?"

"You'll be fine."

"But what if?"

Ms. Wolfe shows up then with Rex and a tall drama student. "We'll get you to a doctor, hon." Her voice is so soothing I can't believe it's her.

"Should I stay with you?" I ask Gigi.

"Caitlin, shouldn't you be onstage for the finale?" Ms. Wolfe asks. "We're starting as soon as we get her offstage. You need all the practice you can get."

Yeah, that's her alright. I mouth, *Call me* to Gigi, and head backstage.

A minute later, we all go onstage to do the finale.

Of course, with Ms. Wolfe gone, I do the whole thing perfectly.

Subj: Worried
Date: 12/11, 1:17 a.m., Eastern Standard Time
To: pippin725@micromail.net
From: Caitlinmcc@dslnet.com

Do you ever wonder what it would be like if you couldn't perform anymore? C

Subj: Re: Worried
Date: 12/11, 3:42 a.m., Eastern Standard Time
To: Caitlinmcc@dslnet.com
From: pippin725@micromail.net

No. I don't let myself think about that even as a theory.
xxoo Sean

*N*o Drama class Friday. Instead, we have extra rehearsal time, and Ms. Wolfe rearranges everyone to accommodate Gigi's absence. Surprise, surprise, I'm still in back. Misty gets Gigi's solo line in the opening number.

"I know her other songs too," she tells Rowena. "The Judy Garland number—I could take her place."

"Hardly," I mutter.

"Actually, we'd already discussed that, Misty," Rowena says. "Would you and Sylvanie be able to come in during lunch and go over it?"

"Absolutely," Misty says. "I'd be honored." She starts back to her place, and I see her mouth, *Yesss!* and pump her fist at Gus.

"Like a turkey buzzard waiting for fresh kill," I mutter to Sean.

Misty hears me and smirks. "Hey, a star is born." She turns back to Rowena. "I could do her other solo too."

"Thanks, Misty. We've taken care of that."

"Just trying to be helpful."

Helpful like a broken leg.

"Thank you, Misty."

By four, there's still no word from Gigi.

"Have you heard anything at all?" I ask Sean over a stale sandwich from The Pit. Most people went home after school, but we both stayed.

"I heard Davis say she had a doctor's appointment this morning," Sean says. "Don't let this ruin it for you. She wouldn't want you to worry about her."

"You make it sound like she's dead."

"No one ever died of a leg injury."

"I think Gigi would rather die than miss a performance—especially if she knew Misty was singing one of her songs."

Before the show, I stand backstage, holding the dress Mom and I bought that day at The Falls, the dress I'm going to wear for my duet. It smells like the store and our day, and I wonder what it's going to be like after today. Will everything change?

Then I'm onstage. I get through the opening okay. During the first-act finale, I look out into the audience. No Mom, of course. She wouldn't have come, even if I'd told her.

Then it's time for our duet. While I'm onstage, I think about:

Breathing in and breathing out.

Expanding my diaphragm. Punching the high notes.

Putting my voice into my head.

Up!

The cough drop I ate.

Violetta. Her love for Alfredo. Her sacrifices and bravery even in death.

Keeping my feet wide enough that I don't fall over.

I don't think about Mom and Arnold or the lies I told Rowena. I don't think about Gigi saying what if she can't dance again.

I just open my throat and let my voice fly to the ceiling.

This is who I am. This is what I love. This is who I am. I know that I can do it, and it's what I want to do more than anything. And I realize I have to do anything I can to make it happen, even if it means leaving other things behind.

We finish our song. The applause is thunderous. I take Sean's hand and stand there, letting it surround us. I know I need to go to the summer program, even if I'm scared. I can do it. This is who I am. I need to talk to Mom, and maybe get her to come to tomorrow's performance. Maybe if she sees it, she'll understand. Somehow.

*C*all it post-game letdown. I have Mom's car, and on the way back home from the performance, I decide to stop at the French bakery for coffee. Tomorrow we're having a big cast party, but tonight, I'm sort of dreading going home to face up to Mom. She'll be all happy after her big date with Arnold, doing some kind of happy-Mom-dance, maybe showing off her engagement ring or committing random acts of lust on our living room sofa. I so can't deal with that. I have a lot of things to think about here.

I'm sitting, drinking a coffee, and reading a free copy of the *New Times* when Nick walks in. Great. He pretends he doesn't see me. Or maybe he *does* see me because he orders his coffee and goes back out to his car. Huge sigh of relief. I can't deal with Nick either. A few minutes later, I finish my coffee and leave too.

But when I get outside, the car won't start. I remember what Mom usually does when that happens, pressing on the gas pedal before she starts the car and stuff, but, like my mother, it doesn't work. It's almost midnight and too late to call a mechanic. Finally, I decide to walk home.

It seemed like an okay idea. But when I start down the road, it suddenly seems a lot farther than when I drive, and it's like every slasher movie I've ever seen. It's after midnight now, and the shadows are moving. Night things rustle in bushes. Two cars slow when they see me, then roar past.

Then another car slows to a crawl and follows me. At first, it's a block behind, the tires crunching across a gravel driveway. I wave to it to pass, but it doesn't. I turn the corner. The car turns too.

I start to run. I'm about to run to the nearest house and bang on the door until they let me in. But then I hear a voice.

"Cat!"

God. How perfect. It's Nick. *Is he stalking me? Did he follow me from the French bakery? Is it good that it's him and not some random pervert, or is it worse?*

I turn. "Leave me alone, Nick."

His interior lights are on, and I see him holding up a hand in mock helplessness. "That's not fair, Cat. I haven't been bothering you." He thinks about it, then amends. "Not for a long time, anyway. You know that's true. I haven't called you since April. I wasn't even going to talk to you tonight. I drank my coffee in the stinking car, so I wouldn't make you nervous. But then I saw you flirting with death out here. You shouldn't be walking at night. There's all kinds of people in the world, drunks who'd run you off the road like you're a target in a computer game. There's lots of guys worse than me out there too, even if you don't believe it." He reaches for the light switch and turns it off. "But hey, you want to walk, walk."

I see the window start to go up, and I realize he's right. I'm still pretty far from home. The night is strange and scary, and you hear all the time about guys who would cut you into little pieces. Nick's not one of those. He's not a rapist either.

"Wait!" I barely get the word out before the window reaches the top.

He doesn't make me wait. I see the window start down immediately. Then the light goes back on, and I can see his face.

"I'm sorry." I walk closer. "I do want a ride. It's nice of you to offer, after . . ."

I don't finish the sentence, but he gestures at the passenger seat, and I get in. My hand sweeps across cool, soft leather, and I think of Sean's junky old car. I catch a glimpse of Nick's face before he turns the light off again. He isn't grinning or anything.

"Should we go back to your car?" he says. "I have jumper cables."

I shake my head. "I'll deal with it tomorrow. But thanks."

We drive in silence a few blocks. Finally, I say, "So why are you out all alone on a Saturday? Where are your friends?"

I can almost hear his shrug. "Don't know. The past few months I haven't related much to those guys. I quit the football team."

I squeak in surprise.

"I just wasn't real good at it, you know. It stressed me, and I'm trying to cut down on things that stress me. Some things, you're just never going to be good at, no matter how hard you try."

I think of dance class. And leaving Key to get away from cheerleading. "Yeah."

"Anyway, since I quit, I don't have that much in common with those guys anymore, other than partying and getting trashed, which I'm also trying to cut down on. I don't feel right with them anymore. Except Tom, I'm still friends with him."

I nod again. I wonder if the changes he's making are because of me. "Yeah. I feel that way all the time."

"You?" He laughs. "Nah, everyone loves you. Me, I'm the smartass."

"I'm not smartass enough at my school. Everyone's so much more exciting than me there."

He shifts his arm on the seat, but doesn't move to touch me. "Yeah, I heard you were going to that arty school. It's really true?"

"Yeah. I wasn't sure about it at first, but now I like it." I get ready for him to say something about how nerdy the school is.

But he says, "That's amazing. I always liked that about you, how you knew what you wanted to do, that singing stuff. I'm not like that about anything yet." He thinks about it. "Maybe writing. I got some stuff published in the school literary journal. Poetry. Maybe I'll be a poet. Ha! My dad would think that's completely stupid—you can't make money being a poet. But he thinks everything I do is stupid."

"I don't. Lots of people . . ." I realize we're driving toward the causeway, off the Key. Where is he taking me? Then I remember what I told everyone. I touch his arm. "Oh, I'm back with my mom now. I didn't . . . it didn't work out with my dad."

He gives a nervous laugh, then slows to make a U-turn. "Didn't work out? Sounds familiar." He looks at my hand, then away. I pull it back to my lap.

"You're dad's still . . . ?" *Still hitting you?*

"Still a jerk? Yeah. He's . . . still him. It's better lately. We had it out over the summer, and he isn't on my case as much as he used to be."

I nod. "I'm glad."

"But it's still . . . strained. I'm marking time until I can go away to college. I'm already collecting brochures. I want to go someplace that'll give me a full ride so I don't have to depend on him. I'm thinking maybe the west coast—Washington State or California."

"Wow. That's so far."

"Yeah, I want far. There's nothing for me here. Besides, it would be cool to go someplace new, try something new—like you did with that school. It was really brave, you leaving everything and going there."

I think of the summer program in New York. Someplace new. "You don't think I was just running away?"

"I don't know. Sounds like you were maybe running *to* something."

"Maybe so." I hadn't thought about it that much, but he's right. I was running—am running—toward opera, toward something that's right for me. We pass under a street lamp, and I see him in the light, the shadows falling across his sharp cheekbones. He is a man of light and shadow, like he always was. I realize I'm leaning closer to him, staring at him and remembering what it was like to have someone like him want me, kiss me. I look away.

"And even if you *are* running away, hell, what's wrong with that when you've got something to run away from? I'm running for sure. I know I don't want to live with my dad, and if I stay here, I might end up like him."

"Like him?" We're on my street. I have two minutes, max, left with him, and the knowledge makes me brave. When he nods, I say, "I don't think so. That's why you took the class again, isn't it? So you wouldn't end up like him?"

"Right. I graduate next week, you know. Or maybe I never really graduate. Maybe I'll always have to think about . . . what happened with you, and spend my whole life making it right. You said you didn't believe me when I said I loved you, when I said I was sorry. But I did love you, Caitlin. I did. I loved you so much, and I screwed up so bad. It took me a while to realize . . . what happened, it was a wake-up call for me. Mario—that's my counselor—he said it was like God kicking me in the butt so I would know I screwed up, and he was right. I hate what I did to you."

"God kicking you in the butt, huh?" We're in my driveway now. The lights are still off, but Mom should be home any second. It's way after midnight. I should run for it, thank him for the ride, and go. It's so close. I say, "I know. Believe me, I know all about not wanting to be that person."

He turns to me and smiles. "Do you?"

"Yeah. Thank you . . . for the ride and for talking to . . ."

My voice goes choky, and then he's kissing me. Or maybe I'm kissing him. I don't know who starts it, but I'm not fighting it. We're kissing, and I'm in his arms.

Finally, we separate. He stares at me. I stare at him.

He speaks first.

"Wow. I wasn't expecting that."

"Me either."

My mind is racing. I'm thinking, *What have I done? What have I done? I transferred schools and spent a whole year trying to stay away from this guy, and I'd just about done it. Just a few days ago, I was saying I didn't need a boyfriend.*

"I'm sorry," he says. "I'm so sorry. I didn't mean for that to happen."

"Nick, I don't think . . ."

"I'm sorry, Caitlin. I think it's a bad idea, you and me. When I offered you a ride, I was just . . . offering you a ride. You have to believe that. I spent so long trying to get over you. I can't go backward."

I gape at him. "You're saying you think it's a bad idea . . . this?"

He looks down. "Yeah. I'm sorry. But I can't let this relationship with you define me."

Define me. I start to laugh. "Oh, thank God. I think so too."

"You do?" He laughs, a nervous laugh.

"Yeah. I don't know. You were there in the moonlight and I guess it's no secret I always thought you were hot, but . . . Oh, god, you're so right." I can't stop laughing like a crazy person.

"Yeah. For the longest time, I was telling myself, You have to move on, man. She doesn't want you. But I never really thought I would. But I can, and I think that's okay, Cat."

"Me either. This is the first time since I broke up with you that I really felt like I *had* broken up with you. I'll always care about you, but you're right."

We sit there another few seconds, laughing. Then he says, "Guess I should go."

I nod and open the door. "Thanks again . . . for the ride. And for everything."

I wonder if Mom's going to pull up any second. She'll freak if she sees me with Nick. But probably, she's too busy being overjoyed about Arnold.

I start toward the door. When I'm almost there, I turn back. "Nick, wait!"

"Yeah?"

I walk back to his car.

"I just want to say . . ." I have no idea what I want to say. "I won't be afraid of you anymore. I'm not the person I was a year ago. I've changed, and so have you."

"Yeah, you're right," he says. "Sing some opera for me someday, huh?"

I nod. I start away from the car, then turn and give him a wave. It will be all right. Mom forgot to turn on the porch light, but between the streetlights and the stars, I can see clearly. I find the key. It will be all right.

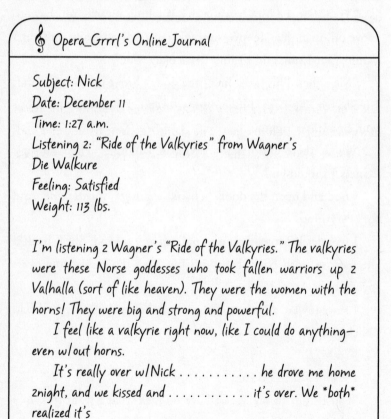

♪ Opera_Grrrl's Online Journal

Subject: Nick
Date: December 11
Time: 1:27 a.m.
Listening 2: "Ride of the Valkyries" from Wagner's
Die Walkure
Feeling: Satisfied
Weight: 113 lbs.

I'm listening 2 Wagner's "Ride of the Valkyries." The valkyries were these Norse goddesses who took fallen warriors up 2 Valhalla (sort of like heaven). They were the women with the horns! They were big and strong and powerful.

I feel like a valkyrie right now, like I could do anything—even w/out horns.

It's really over w/Nick . . . . he drove me home 2night, and we kissed and . . . . it's over. We *both* realized it's

A squeal of brakes in the driveway. Then I hear voices, angry voices.

"Stay away from me!"

I stop typing and run to the window.

It's my mother. She has on the velvet dress from this afternoon, but her shoes are in her hand, and there's yelling as she slams the car door. I catch a few words.

"Get away from me. You stay away, or I'll call the cops!"

"Crazy slut!"

I run downstairs. I open the door just as Mom stumbles in.

"Oh, Caitlin!" Her hair's messy, and she's crying. Her mascara's running down her face. She slams the door behind her and leans on it while I pull the deadbolt. "Oh, Caitlin, you were so right about him!"

I thought it was going to be the perfect evening." We're sitting in my mother's room. I sit at Mom's dressing table like I used to when I was a little kid. Mom paces the floor.

"The opera was at eight. Arnold said he'd pick me up at seven, so we'd have lots of time to walk around. 'See and be seen with my beautiful girl.' That's what he said."

"Mm-hmm." I nod. "That's nice."

"It would have been. Except he didn't show up until twenty to eight. We were late and had to stand outside until the orchestra finished playing its introduction thingy."

"The overture," I say. "Sorry."

"No, that's okay. Anyway, he said he had to work late. Since when do podiatrists work late? And on a Friday? Was there some sort of *bunion* emergency?"

That's probably what Mrs. Arnold thought, all those times when Arnold worked late because he was with Mom. But I control myself.

"At least . . ." She's still pacing, taking the pins out of her hair. It stays hanging at an odd angle, even after most of the pins are out. "We made it for the first act, and—Oh, Caitlin—it was beautiful. The singing. The costumes. For the first time, I understood why you like it so much. I really liked it, honey. Arnold wanted to . . . snuggle during the show."

Translation: He tried to get in her pants right there at the performing arts center.

"But I didn't mind. I was all wrapped up in the story. It was just like that Nicole Kidman movie, the one that takes place at the Moulin Rouge. I didn't even mind too much when he said his ankle hurt and he wanted to stay in our seats during intermission, even though it meant no one would see my dress. I figured he would see it at dinner. As it turned out, we never ate dinner."

"You didn't? Then where were you all this time?"

"Oh, we went to a restaurant all right, but we didn't eat. But I'm getting ahead of the story. Anyway, the second act started, and it was so beautiful, so . . . so noble."

"What was?" I've missed something.

"What Violetta did, Caitlin. Don't you think so? When Alfredo's father tells Vi that his daughter may never be able to marry her beloved because Al's dating a . . . a . . ."

"A hooker."

"Right. And so Vi breaks up with Al, and tells him she doesn't love him even though she does, so his family can be happy. It was so noble, so strong. She was right, but it was sad."

She's crying again. I can't believe my mother's crying about *La Traviata. What's up with that?*

"I know." I actually pat her shoulder. I've never done that in my life. "That's what I love about that opera."

"Violetta is such a good person, and Al doesn't realize . . ." She wipes her eyes with the backs of her hands. "So that got me thinking about Arnold and his family."

"I'm glad you thought about that," I say.

"Me too. So we went to the restaurant, and Arnold said he had something important to discuss with me. And I said I wasn't sure if getting married was a good idea."

"What?"

She nods. "But you know what that man said to me?" When I shake my head, she says, "He wanted me to go on a cruise with him. *That's* what he had to discuss at dinner that was so important. When I said I thought he was going to propose, he actually laughed."

"He laughed?" I'm picturing it, her all dressed up at a fancy restaurant, waiting for him to propose, and I feel *soooo* bad for her, even though I was so mad before.

"Laughed. He said he never planned on marrying me. 'We're just having some fun, Valerie. I'd never leave my wife for someone like you.' Someone like me! That's what he said. Like I'm some . . . some . . ."

I don't finish the sentence for her.

"Some skank! Can you believe that?" she says.

I can believe it because he's scum, but I can't believe he told her. "What did *you* say, Mom?"

"I didn't say a thing." She shakes her hair out. "I threw a lobster at him."

I sit again. It's too much to stand. "A what?"

"A lobster. And two little bowls of drawn butter. I'm positive that's what Violetta would have wanted me to do—I mean, if she was a real person. And as God is my witness, the only regret I have in the whole thing is that that poor creature had to die, only to be thrown at Dr. Arnold Mikloshevsky."

But I'm barely listening at this point. I'm picturing that lobster, sailing—claws out—across an elegant table, attaching itself to Arnold's nose. Then I picture drawn butter dripping off the last remaining strands of Arnold's hair.

For the second time in one night, I start to laugh.

"It's not funny!" Mom yells. "It's not . . . it's!" She smiles. "Okay, a little."

I finally manage to calm down. "I'm sorry. I know you feel bad, but . . . butter?"

We both start laughing hard. When one of us is about to stop, the other one yells, "Butter!" and we both start again.

Finally, I say, "I'm glad, Mom. I'm glad you dumped him. I'm proud of you." I know I should be happy that Mom finally knows what a jerk Arnold is, that her sinister plan was thwarted, and she won't be profiting from Mrs. Arnold's misery, and better yet, that she figured it out for herself. But somehow, standing there in her velvet dress with her mascara messed up and hair all over the place, Mom looks less like a villain, and more like a heroine.

"He insisted on driving me home. I think he was worried that if I got into a cab, I might show up on his doorstep and talk to his wife." She turns her back to me. "Can you unzip this?"

I lean to undo her zipper, and she says it again, those words I've longed to hear all my life. "You were right."

I nod and say, "Wonder how he explained the drawn butter to his wife."

"Yeah, I'd like to have been there for that. But I bet he came up with something, and I bet she believed him. Some women will believe anything." She looks in the mirror and sighs. "Guess that's me, huh?"

"No, of course not."

She shrugs. "It's true. You had to tell me how stupid it was to date that guy. You *and* Violetta." She slips the dress off, and lets it drop to the floor so she's standing there in her strapless bra and underwear. "Time to start over again."

"What?"

"Dating. The hunt." She makes the universal Quotation Mark symbol with her fingers. "*Find a Husband After 35.* That's what I was trying to say that day when I said it scared me when you talked about moving out."

I wince, thinking about that day. "What did you mean?"

"The idea of being alone, it's scary. I've never been alone. I've always had someone—first my parents, then your father, then you. I don't know if I can handle being alone with myself once you leave. It's scary thinking about things changing. I mean, maybe it's not perfect, but it's what I'm used to." She turns away to pick the dress up.

That's just what I did with Rowena and the summer program. I didn't take a chance because I was afraid. "I understand, Mom. Don't worry."

"We should go to bed." She goes to hang up the dress.

I start for the door. "I wish I'd seen it, with the lobster."

"Yeah, it was great."

"Good night, Mommy."

*F*reedom! The next morning when I wake up, I can feel it in the air. Freedom. Freedom from Nick, from Sean, from Arnold—freedom to do whatever I want to do without having to ask anyone's permission, and it's wonderful. So the first thing I do is log onto my journal and start to finish the entry from last night. I'm adding the part about Arnold and the lobster, when there's a knock on the door.

It's Mom. She's holding two manila envelopes. "I wanted you to see something. I was up all night, working on them."

"What are these?"

"I think you'll be able to figure it out. You're a smart girl. Why don't you look at them. I'll give you a makeover, if you want. But later."

I nod and take the envelopes. I sit on the bed and take out the first one. It's from Mom's accountant, Mr. Lowman: a letter and last year's tax return. I don't know why she's showing me this. I have no clue how to read a tax return. But I flip through it.

On the first page, there's a section that says INCOME. Lines with numbers. The highest number is on the line that says BUSINESS INCOME and I practically fall off the bed when I see it. I had no idea Mom made that much. *Is this all from real estate, or does that include her business of sponging off Dad?*

I check out the line marked ALIMONY.

The number on that line is 0.

Point for Mom. But is child support the same as alimony, or is it separate somewhere? I flip through the rest of the form and find nothing about child support. Then I see that the second envelope says CHILD SUPPORT in Mom's round, girlish handwriting. She's written in purple and dotted the I with a circle.

Inside is a Post-it note from Mom that says CAITLIN, CHILD SUPPORT ISN'T INCLUDED ON THE TAX RETURN. LUCKY ME. It's attached to copies of Dad's child support checks. I recognize that handwriting too—his wife, Macy's.

The second thing I notice about the checks are the amounts—they would *maybe* pay for my clothes if I didn't wear anything extravagant like, say, sneakers. I remember the big deal Dad made about paying for my voice lessons. If you subtracted that amount, the check is practically nothing.

The third thing I notice is that the checks are always late. Sometimes two or three months at a time, and every one is signed by Macy.

I slip all the papers back into their envelopes.

I find Mom in her room. She's putting on her makeup. In

times of distress, it's always makeup. I slide the envelopes over by the mirror.

"How about that makeover?" I say.

She pulls out a bottle. "Wash up first. I have this new cleanser." She hands it to me. "And moisturizer. You need to moisturize, even when you're young—to trap in the moisture and prevent damage. I wish I'd known that when I was your age. There are so many things I wish I'd known, but that one I think of every time I look in a mirror."

I start to repeat the line about how there's always Botox, but instead, I say, "You're mad about what I said that day, about leeching off Dad."

"Not mad." She hands me the moisturizer. "Sad, a little. You were thinking it for a long time, weren't you?"

"Years. But I thought Dad . . . I thought . . ."

"He used to pay alimony. We agreed I was going to be a stay-at-home mother. But then he married Macy and they contested the agreement. So I got my real estate license and started selling Emma Leigh. I liked those things anyway. They were fun, and with my looks and personality, I was good at them."

I nod. It always comes down to her looks. Is that because she feels like that's all she has? Scary thought. I finish with the cleanser and start moisturizing.

"Lance was still paying pretty much child support at that point—not enough, but something." She looks at me and moves my hands away from my face. "No, no, honey. Like this. An upward motion, with the thumbs. The idea is to gently massage away any future wrinkles." She works the moisturizer in like I'm one of her Emma Leigh clients. "But any time I'd start earning a little more, he'd come to me, wanting to make the payments lower. I think Macy saw my picture in the real estate ads. Never mind that real estate's an iffy business. Never mind that Key Biscayne is an expensive place to live—we could always move someplace cheaper, as Lance pointed out constantly. Never mind that you were his *child* for God's sake, and he should *want* to support you and *want* you to live someplace nice."

I wince. Dad never *wanted* to pay for anything for me. Even I knew that.

Mom continues. "Finally, I asked him what he was willing to pay, and we settled on an amount that was maybe a quarter of what he should have been paying."

"Why?"

"Sometimes you get tired of fighting." She hands me a bottle. "Okay, now you're ready to get started. I always make my clients do it themselves, so they learn how."

I start to apply the foundation, with an upward motion like she suggested. "Why didn't you tell me?"

"I guess I thought it was better if you didn't know what a jerk your father was."

"I think I always knew, but *jerk* isn't the word I'd use."

She laughs. "Right. And you thought I was a jerk because you thought I sponged off him." She hands me a blush. "Excellent job on the foundation, by the way. You have such beautiful skin—such tiny pores."

"Thanks." I take the blush from her and start to sweep it on. "I wish I'd known."

"I didn't want you to. But I don't want you thinking I'm lazy either."

I apply the blush, and she nods that I did it right. "But Arnold. You acted like you needed him for support."

She pushes her hand through her hair. "It's always such a struggle to pay for the upkeep of this house. But it's the only home you've ever known. I worry about college too. Your father's child support stops completely when you hit eighteen."

I look around her room, and think about our house. She was willing to put up with Dr. Toe-Jam just to stay here? For me?

"I might get a scholarship," I say. "There are scholarships for music."

I wait for her to say something awful about how you can't count on those things. But instead, she says, "Well, we can hope."

I finish with the blush and start with eye shadow. "Which colors do you think?"

She points to a small case. "This one's the base, for the entire lid. And then this one's for the brow line, and this one's for the crease. It gives you the extra definition you need." She points to a couple of colors. "And . . ."

"What else?" I say, assuming she means another eye shadow.

"Oh, I don't know. I guess it felt . . . nice having someone like that, someone wealthy, wanting me like that. He made me feel . . ." She shrugs.

I remember the feeling I always had, walking arm-in-arm with Nick at school.

"Valuable," I say, brushing on the base eye shadow. "He made you feel valuable."

She nods. "Yeah. I guess that's it."

I say, "I think that you are way too valuable for Arnold Mikloshevsky and his clammy hands."

She nods. "I know you're right. But sometimes it's hard to believe that. It's so hard to find someone who loves you for yourself, and not just because you're pretty or act the way they want you to act."

I think of Sean. I have that with him. Yes, he's a friend, but he's a good friend.

"Are you okay?" I say.

She nods. "I think I'm getting better." She takes out a different lipstick and holds it near my face, then recaps it. "Oh, Caitlin, he really was a toady little man, wasn't he? Every time he kissed me, I'd think, *Valerie McCourt, has it really come to this?*"

I giggle, then stop myself. "He kept looking at my boobs."

"Mine too—and he had some boobs of his own, let me tell you!"

I can't suppress the giggle that comes after that, and Mom joins right in.

"Mom?" I say after a minute. "I wish . . . I have a performance tonight at school."

She raises an eyebrow like, *Were you going to tell me about it?*

"Yeah," I say. "I thought you were too busy with Arnold, so I didn't . . ." I know that's not really true. "I'm sorry. I just didn't tell you. But it's at eight tonight, and I'm wearing the dress you bought me, and I wish you'd come."

"I wouldn't miss it." She looks at the blush I've put on. "And maybe I could help you out with your makeup for it too."

I nod. Things with Mom will never be perfect. They are what they are. But even when times are hard, we'll always have makeup just like when I was little. Cosmetics are the glue that binds us together. But maybe we can have a bit more.

Sean and I sing our duet the best we've ever sung it. Maybe the best I've ever sung *anything*. For once I sound like an opera singer to my own ears, and I know that this is what I want—to be a diva, to stand onstage and make other people hear this music the way *I* hear it, not as something old and faded, but as something alive, forever and ever. And I'll do anything—including telling Mom I need to spend the summer in New York and trying and auditioning and taking a chance on not making it—to get there.

Sean kisses me on the cheek when we take our bow. Then I run backstage to change for the finale and sit in the darkened wings listening to Gigi singing her solo. Gigi came back today with her leg in a cast (but scheduled to heal up) and ruined Misty's night by saying she could do her Judy Garland number. They cut her dance routine. Instead, she's singing a ballad. It floats backstage to where I'm sitting in the gray darkness. I'm so glad I *can* perform. I have a chance.

After the finale, Rowena catches me backstage. "You were incredible."

"Thanks. I'm really happy."

"I saw your mom in the audience. That's great that she came."

Now is the moment when I should pretend intense interest in makeup removal. But instead, I face Rowena. "Yeah. I wanted to talk to you about that."

"About what?"

"About New York. I lied when I said I asked my mom and she said no. I never asked. I'm sorry."

"What? Why not?"

"A lot of reasons. Stupid ones. Being afraid, maybe. But that's over now, and I really want to go, and I think she'll let me. I'll talk to her about it this time. I promise."

Rowena's concerned expression has changed, and she's staring at something behind me. I turn and realize she's looking at Mom. "I guess we'll find out."

Mom is rushing toward me. She's removed her jacket to reveal a glittery, tight T-shirt. She's yelling, "Baby! Oh, baby, how could you not have told me about this?"

"I'm sorry," I say. I'm apologizing to everyone today. "I'm glad you made it."

"I got the car jump-started. And I had to ask my friend, Linda, to take over my open house. But I wouldn't have missed it. You were so beautiful! And *La Traviata*." She turns to Rowena. "That's my very favorite opera in the world."

I gesture toward Rowena. "Mom, you remember my voice teacher."

Mom smiles her classic Valerie McCourt smile, the one on the real estate signs. "Of course. It's Rowena, right?"

"Right, and . . ."

"Well, I have to congratulate you. You've done an incredible job with her. She's improved. A *lot*." I feel a flicker of annoyance. I push it aside.

Meanwhile, Rowena's stammering, "Er . . ."

"When she was a little girl, she used to sing around the house all the time, and it got so I could barely think straight from all the racket. But now . . . you are one incredible teacher."

Okay, more than a flicker.

"Thank you. Caitlin's a wonderful student."

"And may I add," Mom says, "that you have the loveliest coloring. I can make that gray thing work for you, and if you'd like to set up an appointment, I could show you some creams that would fluff those fine lines right out."

Okay. Way, *way* more than a flicker. *Stop talking, Mom.*

But Rowena's still being gracious. "Maybe so. Can you come before Caitlin's voice lesson next week, then stay and listen to her? I have been thinking I don't devote enough effort to my beauty routine."

"Honey, you can never be too young or too old for proper skin care. Skin is like a child. It needs nurturing. Nourishment."

Rowena nods. "I'm so glad you phrased it that way because

there's another thing that requires nurturing. A talent like Caitlin's needs a place where it can grow. So perhaps *while* we're doing the consultation, I can tell you about an excellent summer program I've suggested to her. I understand she hasn't mentioned it to you yet, but . . ."

They keep talking. I remove my stage makeup. They're doing fine without me. Maybe some things about Mom aren't as annoying to other people as they are to me. Maybe part of the reason she's a successful sales person is she's outgoing and charming.

"Well, it would be hard for me, being alone all summer," Mom's telling Rowena, and I accidentally stick a finger into my eye from the surprise. "But it sounds like a wonderful program, and I guess I'll have to get used to it, if she's going to go away to college soon."

Rowena laughs. "Yeah, I'm an empty-nester myself now. This program could even help Caitlin to get a college scholarship."

"That would be great," Mom says. "I never finished college myself. It's something I always regretted."

She looks away, a little sad. I never thought of my mom as having regrets. I always assumed she got what she wanted—the guy, the house, the free ride. It never occurred to me she might have wanted to be something other than just my mom.

I think about what Miss Davis said, the day Gigi and I did the *Glass Menagerie* scene. *Do you think Amanda ever had any dreams?* I wonder if Mom did.

Subject: Dreams
Date: December 12
Time: 9:13 a.m.
Listening 2: "O Mio Babbino Caro" ("Oh, My
Beloved Daddy") (Have you noticed that there are
never any *mothers* in opera?)
Weight: 114 lbs.

When my mom was young, she wanted 2 be a fashion designer.
She was going 2 regular college, but then she got a scholarship
offer at a big design school in NYC. She was going 2 transfer
her sophomore year. She wanted 2 go 2 Paris 2.

Then she met my dad @ a frat party. They fell in love
("As in love as you can get at a frat party . . . . which
apparently isn't very," she said). She got pregnant and
dropped out of college 2 get married. I already know the rest
of the story.

Anyway, we talked abt. that & then we started talking
abt. my dreams, abt. how I want 2 be a singer. And now that
she understands that I really *do* have talent, that I have a
shot @ it, she's actually being nice abt. it. "I just hope you
don't get your heart broken like mine. They say there's a
broken heart for every light on Broadway. Or wherever they
sing opera."

But I told her my heart might break if I *don't* at least
try. And she seemed 2 get that. We talked abt. the opera

program in New York, and once she found out it wouldn't cost a lot of $$, she said I can send an audition tape. And I can go, if I get in! And I think she actually *wants* me 2 get in! And I think I will!!!! Can you believe it???

I sit by Sean and Gigi at lunch. We've been talking about the cast party, which was pretty wild. (Highlight: Rex declared his love for me and said he'd even learn to sing opera if I wanted him to. He's been learning *"Caro Mio Ben."*) I'm eating a salad with chicken on it, and Gigi hasn't found it necessary to comment on that.

"I was hoping you could help me out with something," I tell them.

"I'm all ears," Sean says.

I tell them about the summer program. "I wasn't sure if I wanted to go, but now I think I do." I look at Sean. "I know you're super-busy getting ready for college auditions, but I was hoping maybe you could help me practice."

Gigi has her leg in a cast. She told me it was a good thing because it keeps her from kicking Misty's butt for trying to get her solo. "That sounds incredible," she says. "Of course you have to go."

"I'll miss the choral camp," I say. "And I wish I could be with you guys."

"We'll be here in the fall," she says. "If I had an opportunity like this, I'd drop you so fast . . ."

I laugh. "At least you're honest."

And I realize that yeah, she really is. That's the thing about having real friends like Gigi and Sean. You feel like you can tell them the truth about stuff in your life, and they won't rag on you or try and use it against you, or try to talk you out of it because it doesn't fit with what they want. If I'd never come to this school, I wouldn't have ever had that.

Sean says, "The program sounds incredible."

"If I don't get in, I'll go to choral camp with you guys."

"You'll get in," Sean says. "With a coach like me, you'll nail your auditions."

I grin at him. The lunchtime conga line is snaking around the cafeteria again. Gus, at its head, yells, "Hey, Diva! Nice job in Drama today."

Misty hits him on the shoulder, but he makes the line swirl around our table and comes back. "Are you ever going to join us?" he asks me. "Conga-ing, I mean?"

"I don't . . . I . . ."

"*Anyone* can conga. It's just . . ." Gus mimes an exaggerated maraca shake as he dances away.

I look at Sean and Gigi. "How about it?"

Sean shrugs. "Why not?"

Gigi says, "I think my orthopedist would have some big reasons why not for me. But you two go."

I stand and hold out my hand to Sean. "Shall we?"

He takes it, and we run to catch up with the conga line.

*L*ots of girls I know like to say they're divas. "I'm such a diva!" they say, while they're rubbing your nose in some five-hundred-dollar shoes their daddy bought them, or whatever. But a diva's a lot more than most sixteen-year-old rich grrrls can comprehend. I plan to be a diva someday—the real kind who sings and gets flowers thrown onstage. But first, I have to make the perfect audition tape.

So I do.

♪ Opera_Grrrl's Online Journal

Subject: Summer Opera Program in New York—Accepted!
Date: April 10
Time: 2:13 p.m.
Listening 2: "Brindisi" from La Traviata
Feeling: Ecstatic
Weight: 115 lbs.

YESSSSSS!!
!!!!!!!!!!!!!!!!!!!!!!!!!!!!!!!!!!